Ill-Served

Susan J. Kroupa

Books by Susan J. Kroupa

The Doodlebugged Mysteries

Bed-Bugged

Out-Sniffed

Dog-Nabbed

Bad-Mouthed

Ruff-Housed

Mis-Chipped

Ill-Served

A Most Magical Christmas

TreeTalker

Copyright © 2021 by Susan J. Kroupa
All rights reserved.

This is a work of fiction. Names, characters, places and incidents are either the products of the author's imagination or are used fictitiously. Any resemblance to actual persons (living or dead), events, or locations is entirely coincidental.

ISBN: 978-0-9985700-4-4
Published by Laurel Fork Press
Laurel Fork, Virginia
https://www.laurelforkpress.com

Photo and Cover Credits:
Labradoodle: © 2016 by Susan J. Kroupa
Cover Design by Susan J. Kroupa
Book Design by Marny K. Parkin

*To the legitimate service dogs everywhere
and those who train them . . .*

Contents

An Unexpected Visitor	7
Family Dispute	19
Moving In	31
Searching	41
Settling In	49
Spoofed!	57
Getting to Know the Neighbors	67
Practice, Practice, Practice	77
Intruder!	93
Good and Bad Encounters	105
Packing It All Up	121
I Do! and No Way!	133
Unwelcome Surprises	143
Home Away from Home	151

The Scene of the Crime	157
True Detectives	167
Rehab	177
Problem Solving	187
Homecomings	193
Undercover	205
Surprise Beginning	213
Happy Endings	223
About the Author	241
Acknowledgments	243
The Doodlebugged Mysteries	245

Chapter 1

An Unexpected Visitor

I

T'S A MIXED-ZONE NEIGHBORHOOD," THE BOSS SAYS, slowing the van as we turn onto a side street. "Apartment buildings and some duplexes, but still lots of single homes."

"And that's it!" The boss points to a house with a large tree in front, and several more in the back. A little strip of lawn behind the sidewalk separates it from the street. Not lawn, really, but mostly weeds.

"The backyard is a lot bigger," the boss says, as he pulls the van into the driveway. Good thing. Hardly room for a dog to pee in the front.

"Only one bathroom, but it's a big one, and there are three bedrooms." He presses the buttons that make the windows all go down.

Molly jumps out, puts me on my leash and gets me out of the crate. I shake and take in the warm moist air. We're here to see the new place we're going to move into because the boss and Annie are getting married.

"What do you think, Doodle?" Molly asks.

I work my nose, taking in the scents. Cats, of course. There doesn't seem to be a neighborhood in the city without cats. And car exhaust. Like the scent of cats, it's everywhere we go. The house smells dusty, with a hint of mildew, along with the distinctive scents of old wood.

The boss leads us up several wooden steps. One of them is badly cracked and another tilts under the weight of my paws. There are a few gaps in the slats on the porch.

"Needs some repair," the boss says, always one to state the obvious, "but nothing we can't do."

"I love it!" Molly exclaims.

The boss's mouth twitches. "You haven't seen it yet. You love that it's only a couple of blocks away from the Franklins."

"A block and a half," Molly says, her face lit up. She runs a hand along a water-stained plastic lawn chair. There are several on the porch.

The Franklins are our very good friends, and Tanya Franklin is Molly's very *best* friend. They like to say they're sisters separated at birth, a statement that doesn't make sense to me because Tanya and her whole family are black and Molly likes to say that she's a hybrid like a labradoodle—half white, half Mexican.

The boss fits a key into the lock and turns it. "Mrs. Thomas will be by in a little bit to bring me the contract, but she was nice enough to have Lamar lend us his key. He keeps an eye on the place."

The door creaks open to reveal a large living room furnished with an old couch and several chairs. A flood of scents hits my nose. More dust, more mildew, and—something darts from behind one of the chairs. Without thinking I lunge after it, ripping the leash from Molly's hand. It veers through the doorway, skittering into what turns out to be the kitchen. Just as I'm closing the gap, it leaps up on the counter and from there to the top of the stove.

"Doodle!" Molly and the boss shout simultaneously, their footsteps thumping on the wood floor.

"Was that a rat?" wails Molly.

Not a rat, which they would have known instantly if they had decent noses.

She turns into the kitchen, the boss right beside her. "It's a *cat!*"

Like I said, can't get away from cats. This one looks young. And half-starved. And ready to do battle if I get too close.

The boss grabs my leash and yanks me toward him, more forcefully than necessary. He glares at me. Okay, admittedly it wasn't my best moment. A Canine Good Citizen, which I recently passed the tests to become, does not rip the leash away from his handler. But, well, dogs were meant to chase and that's a fact.

"Not a cat, a *kitten!* And really pretty. Tricolored." Molly's voice instantly changes. "Here, kitty-kitty," she coos, approaching the stove. The kitten, hair-raised, hisses at me and then starts mewling in a pitiful high voice.

"Poor kitty-kitty." Molly extends her hand. "Poor kitty."

"Don't get scratched," the boss advises.

Molly nods. The kitten turns to her, tense, but doesn't move when Molly gently strokes her head. Before long, Molly picks her up.

"Friendly," the boss says. "Not feral. I wonder if it belongs to someone. Male or female?"

Female, of course. Again, if humans had decent noses . . .

"A girl!" Molly declares after a brief search. The kitten starts to purr.

"She's nice," Molly says. "Maybe if no one claims her, we could keep her."

The boss rubs his beard. "Maybe," he says surprising me, as the boss is generally one to say no. Although, now that I think about it, not as much anymore. Not sure why. Molly looks surprised as well.

"But we'll have to make sure no one owns her."

Molly nods. "I know. I could ask Tanya. She'll know if anyone has a lost kitten. But—" she examines the kitten "—she's awfully thin, so she's been lost for a while."

"We need to find out how she got in. This place was supposed to be locked up. If a kitten could get in, so could a rat, or maybe a squirrel. Or," he says in a voice filled with dread, "a skunk."

This is more the boss I know, worrying about things that can go wrong. There are no rats, squirrels, or skunks in the house that I can smell, and, frankly, if I can't smell them, they're not here.

Holding my leash in a tight grip, the boss leads me around the kitchen while he checks the windows and then into a small room with a back door. The room has coat hooks on one side and a washer and dryer on the other.

"It's got a small mud room," he says.

I don't see any mud. Dust, yes, in great quantities, but no mud, so I'm not sure what he means.

He opens the door and steps through. "And this is the backyard." He holds an arm out to the trees, his eyes glowing with pride.

Whoa. This yard is easily twice as big as ours and has two broad, thick-trunked trees shading it.

"Wow!" Molly says, her eyes round. She strokes the kitten, who has settled comfortably in her arms, although it still watches me cautiously.

"Plenty of room for Doodle and Chloe." The boss studies the yard, smiling. "We'll have to fix the fence, of course, but Lamar doesn't think it will take too much to make it secure."

Lamar is Tanya's father. Mr. Franklin to Molly and me, but the boss calls him Lamar.

He turns and peers at the back door. "Still don't see where the cat got in."

We go back inside, and the boss leads us through the rest of the house. "Three bedrooms," he says, ushering us into one good-sized room. "This will be yours."

"Bigger than mine right now," Molly says, nodding with approval. The kitten continues to purr.

"As I said, only one bathroom." The boss gestures to a bathroom on the other side of Molly's room. "It's old, but functional. I'm going to ask Mrs. Thomas if we can put down new tile if we buy the tile ourselves." He pulls open the shower curtain. "And clean the mold from the grout on those tiles."

"One bathroom is enough," Molly says.

"It's actually a good thing because otherwise we wouldn't be able to afford this place. Everyone wants at least two bathrooms these days. Mrs. Thomas told me she had several lookers who turned it down because of that."

"I love it!" Molly says fervently.

The boss grins at her. "I do, too. And we're lucky to get it. If it weren't for Lamar, I don't think we would have. I'm pretty sure Mrs. Thomas gave us a price break because of his recommendation. And because I said I could fix the fence and do some of the repairs myself." He stops and rubs his beard. "Wish we could buy it. There are a lot of things that need fixing. No air conditioning, for one. We'll have to get window units for the bedrooms if we want to be able to sleep."

He opens a small high window in the bathroom. "Musty in here. I think the place needs a good airing out."

Molly shifts the kitten to one arm, and pulls out her phone, flipping it open and punching a key. Molly likes to say she's the last person on earth to own a flip phone, which is smaller than most of the phones I see. She wants what she calls a "smart" phone, though I don't see how a piece of plastic could be smart. But the boss insists that smart phones aren't good for kids. He says the only reason she has a phone at all is so she can get hold of him when he's at work. All I can say is that she uses it for a lot more than that.

I might have mentioned that I don't really understand phones—how someone right beside me can talk to someone far away. Mysterious, to be sure. The good thing is that dogs have much better hearing than humans, so I can usually know who Molly is talking to and generally follow the conversation. Unlike texts. When Molly texts, all I hear is the beep of her phone, yet somehow she "talks" with it. With texts, I never know what's going on.

This time, Molly has called Tanya.

"Hey!" Tanya's voice comes over the line. "Do you like it?"

"I love it!" Molly exclaims, and the boss glances her way, his grin widening. Have I mentioned that he's been strangely happy recently? Molly says it's because he's getting married.

"And guess what? We found a kitten inside the house!" Molly tells her about the kitten. Molly and Tanya pretty much tell each other everything all the time. Usually more than once, too, if you catch my drift. Humans like to repeat things.

The boss, his hand still tight on the leash, leads me through the house, opening windows in every room to "air it out."

Then we go back through the kitchen to the mudroom. "How did that cat get in?" He frowns, biting his lower lip, staring at the room. And then, "Of course!" He goes over to the dryer, which smells strongly of rusting metal and mold, and pulls it out slightly. Behind it, a hole gapes in the wall.

I stick my nose in it and sniff. Sure enough, it smells of the kitten, as well as lint, rust, and dirt.

"The dryer vent," he says. "Should have thought of that sooner. I'll need to stuff some rags in that until we get our washer and dryer over here and plug up the vent."

Molly, off the phone now, comes in and stares at the washer and dryer. "Those are seriously old. I'm glad we have ours. Tanya's walking over to see the kitten." She gazes down at the bundle in her arms, smiling.

"Okay." The boss still has his head down, inspecting the vent.

"Tanya said she hasn't heard of anyone missing a kitten but could ask at church. But I don't think anyone owns her because she's so thin. We'll need to take her to the vet."

The boss glances up, his eyebrows raised, but merely nods. He goes into the kitchen, ties my leash to a cupboard handle, and then rummages around under the kitchen sink. "Aha!" he says, pulling out a few rags and part of a box. He stuffs them into the hole in the mud room, then looks at it critically. "Not good enough."

The sound of footsteps startles me and I let out a surprised bark. But then I hear Tanya calling. Molly rushes out to meet her. Of course, I'm stuck on the leash in the kitchen. Not good, because unless the boss and I are working, my place is usually with Molly.

Fortunately, the girls come back to the kitchen, chattering all the way. The boss likes to say they talk a mile a minute, which means really fast.

Hey, Tanya's holding the kitten. I pull towards Molly. When neither the boss nor Molly notices, I give another bark, this one short and high.

Molly laughs. "Oh, Doodle, are you feeling left out?" She unties my leash and strokes me under my chin. Much better. I sniff her arms and chest, which, sadly, reek of kitten.

"Don't get too close!" Tanya warns. She steps away from Molly and me. "Doodle makes her nervous. I can feel her claws."

The boss turns to Molly. "I have a bucket of rags in the van. Will you get them?"

Molly nods and we go outside.

Tanya follows us, dropping into one of the dusty chairs on the porch. "Cooler out here," she says.

"Yeah," Molly agrees. She opens the backend of the van and lifts out the rag bucket. "Dad says we need to get air conditioners." She tells Tanya to wait, and we—because I'm still on leash—run into the house and give the boss the bucket. Then we come back outside, and Molly sinks into a chair beside Tanya.

Soon they're talking about someone in their class at school. Not a subject that interests me, but there's plenty to keep my nose busy. Mild air, a slight breeze bringing a buffet of scents to my nose. Except for the kitten, this is a wonderful day.

Tanya suddenly straightens up, looking down the street. A boy and a dog come towards us.

"There's Jordan Taylor," she says. "I forgot he lived near here."

Molly gives her a puzzled look.

"He's a nice kid. Goes to our church. A couple of years older than me." Tanya watches the boy a minute. "I didn't know he'd gotten his dog."

"Dog?" Molly asks.

"Yeah. A service dog. Jordan has Type 1 Diabetes. The dog is supposed to warn him if his blood sugar goes too low. You should meet him." She jumps up and walks quickly to the sidewalk. "Jordan," she calls, waving.

Molly and I follow.

The boy waves back. And then, half-dragged by the large yellow Lab he has on leash, comes over to us.

"Hey," he says in a soft, almost shy, voice. He's taller than Tanya, and just as thin and he has the same black curly hair—much like my own—and dark eyes.

"You *got* him!" Tanya says.

"Yeah." Jordan smiles, tightening the leash a little as the dog strains toward me. "Last Wednesday. His name is Cooper. He's really nice."

Tanya touches Molly's arm. "This is Molly. She's moving into Mrs. Thomas's house in a few weeks."

Molly smiles. "Nice to meet you, Jordan. And you, Cooper." She stretches out a hand and pets the dog, then gestures to me. "And this is Doodle. Maybe they can play together."

I move closer to sniff noses. Cooper tugs forward and tries to bow.

"Cooper!" Jordan exclaims. He jerks the leash a little.

Molly pulls me back behind her. "He just wants to play."

"Yeah," Jordan agrees. "Mama says he's still sort of a puppy. He's only a year and a half old."

"Really?" Molly frowns. "That's pretty young for a service dog."

"I guess. His trainer says it's better if he's young because I'll have him a longer time. 'Cause dogs don't live as long as people."

"I know, right?" Molly agrees. "Annie says a dog's greatest flaw is that they don't live long enough."

I have no idea what they're talking about. All the dogs I know are alive.

"And he says because I'm thirteen he'll be with me until I go to college." Jordan leans down and pets Cooper, who licks his hand.

"Poor puppy." Tanya leans toward Cooper, using that baby voice people sometimes use with dogs. And kittens. Can't say I like it, although it's not as bad as people patting me on the head. "Do all these new things bother you?"

Suddenly, I hear growling. The kitten! She yowls and hisses at Cooper. "Ouch!" Tanya stumbles backward as the kitten frantically climbs up her blouse, then arcs to the ground and dashes toward the front door.

With a roar, Cooper lunges forward, tearing the leash from Jordan's hand.

Everyone shouts at once. The kitten makes it to the door and claws to the top of the screen. Cooper, barking madly, leaps after her, but falls short.

Tanya reaches the door first. She grabs Cooper's leash and tries to pull him away. "No!" she shouts. Cooper, still barking, struggles against the leash. Tanya staggers forward, unable to hold him back.

"What's going on?" The boss opens the screen door, the kitten still attached, and steps outside. He grabs Cooper's leash from Tanya and drags the dog down the steps and off the porch.

"No!" he bellows. And then, "Sit!"

Cooper, suddenly chastened, sits, his eyes on the boss. For a moment, no one speaks.

The boss takes a deep breath. "What happened?"

Tanya says, "I got too close to Cooper and the kitten freaked out. And then Cooper chased her." She blinks hard. "It's my fault. I got too close. I forgot. I'm so sorry, Jordan," she says turning towards him.

"It's okay." Jordan's eyes are wide and his whole body stiff. "But I better take him home now." He goes over to the boss, who hands him the leash.

"Keep a tight grip," the boss says.

Jordan nods emphatically. "I will. Come on Cooper, let's go home."

Cooper jumps up and, forging ahead, leads the way down the road.

Tanya goes to the screen door. "Here, kitty-kitty." She tries to take the kitten, but it hangs on tightly. "Here kitty-kitty."

"Cooper doesn't act much like a service dog," Molly says in a low voice. Her eyes are on Jordan and Cooper.

Come to think of it, he doesn't. He didn't even have the manners of a Canine Good Citizen, which I may have mentioned I recently became. And service dogs are supposed to have better manners than that. They're supposed to be the most obedient dogs of all. Which is why, frankly, a service dog career didn't work out for me. Not my thing, waiting for orders every minute of the day. I prefer searching for bed bugs. We have our work, the boss and me, and then we're done. And I can be with Molly. Much better that way. I touch my nose to Molly's hand.

But she doesn't seem to notice. She's staring at Jordan and Cooper now a block away, her hand clenched tightly on my leash, her face lined with worry. "He doesn't act like a service dog at all."

Chapter 2

Family Dispute

WE STAY ON THE PORCH, MOLLY, TANYA, AND ME, waiting for the landlady, Mrs. Thomas. The boss is inside, writing down a list of repairs he'd like to do. The kitten, calmer now, purrs in Tanya's arms, which I prefer to having Molly hold her. She still watches me warily whenever I move, but doesn't hiss any more.

"I bet that's her," Tanya says, pointing at an older sedan, long and low to the ground, moving slowly toward us.

But the car continues past our house. The driver is a bald man whose head barely extends above the steering wheel.

"Not sure he should be on the road!" Tanya says. "He's ancient!"

We wait awhile longer while Molly and Tanya discuss names for the kitten.

"Not that one!" Molly says, nodding at a small car zipping toward us. "Can't imagine her driving a hybrid."

Lost me there, but I don't have time to think about it because the little car whips into the driveway and parks beside our van. A woman with short white hair, curly like my own, sits behind the wheel.

"And I was wrong," Molly says under her breath.

The girls jump up and we all walk quickly over to the car, which carries all sorts of interesting odors. I sniff tires that have been peed on by several dogs. Molly tightens the leash a little as I start to lift my leg. "Doodle," she warns in a low voice. Molly doesn't like me to pee on car tires and the boss absolutely hates it. Disappointing, because I'd love to add my scent to the ones here.

"Hi," Molly says as the woman steps out of the car. She's not quite as tall as the boss, but almost, and has dark eyes like Tanya. She's wearing sandals, those pants that are tight and stop mid-leg, and a loose print blouse.

Molly extends a hand. "I'm Molly Hunter. Are you Mrs. Thomas?"

"The one and the same." Mrs. Thomas shakes Molly's hand, and then turns to Tanya. "And how is your family doing? Missed your mother last week at church."

Tanya nods. "She had to work. We're all fine. Excited that the Hunters are going to live closer to us. Molly is my best friend."

"And what have we got here?" Mrs. Thomas reaches over to pet the kitten.

Molly explains how they found her. "Dad says we might be able to keep her if we can't find her family. But only if you don't mind. We absolutely won't do anything you don't want us to."

I'm not sure why everyone is so interested in this kitten. I mean, seriously. I bump my nose against Molly's leg.

"And this is Doodle," Molly says, taking the hint. "He's a certified bed bug dog."

Mrs. Thomas raises her eyebrows. "I guess we'll never have to worry about getting an infestation here, will we?" She bends down to give me a pat. "Hello, Mr. Doodle."

"He's also a Canine Good Citizen, so you won't have to worry about him in the house or anything," Molly says.

Tanya adds, "He has to pass all sorts of tests to be a bed bug dog and he never gets in trouble."

Seriously? Not sure the boss would agree.

Molly nods. "And Annie—she's the one Dad's marrying—is a dog trainer. She's super good with dogs and her beagle Chloe is really well-trained. Maybe even better than Doodle."

What? I don't think so. Unless by well-trained you mean obedient, which, as I've already mentioned, is *not* the same thing.

"So you don't have to worry about us." Molly reaches down to touch my head.

The screen door opens and the boss hurries over. "Worry?" he asks, a frown starting above his eyes.

Mrs. Thomas, her face creased in a smile, says, "I have the testimony of two very earnest girls, a dog, and a kitten, that you will be good renters and I have no reason to worry."

The boss looks momentarily confused, but then introduces himself and we all head toward the porch.

"Oh." Mrs. Thomas goes back to her car, reaches inside, and pulls out a slim briefcase. "Got the contract," she says. She starts back and then stops, gazing upward. "This tree wasn't very big when Raymond and I moved in." She shakes her head. "So many memories." She turns her face toward us. "I still miss him every single day, you know. We were so thrilled the day we moved in. A dream come true to have a real home, not just an apartment. We felt richer than a Rockefeller."

Not sure what that is, but the boss nods. "I know what you mean. This is a *great* place. Big trees, big yard, large rooms."

"We love it!" Molly adds.

Mrs. Thomas smiles, but her eyes are on the yard. "Well, I've let it decline, that's for sure." She shakes her head. "Look at that poor sorry strip of . . . I don't think it can be called lawn anymore. Never could get it to grow well once the tree got bigger, but now . . ." she shakes her head again. "If I don't watch it, I'll end up a slum landlord."

"No," the boss says. "I mean there are repairs to be done, for sure, and I've made a list of what I'd like to do—if you agree, of course—but it's miles away from a slum."

"A list!" She nods approvingly. "Lamar said I'd like you, and he's right. Well, let's go see what needs to be done and—" she holds up the briefcase "—get this done."

We all troop into the house. The boss leads Mrs. Thomas from room to room pointing out repairs he'd like to make. "I won't be able to afford to do it all at once, but Lamar and his sons have offered to help with the labor and Annie's good with a hammer as well. A little at a time." He meets her eyes. "We will be good renters," he promises. "We'll keep the place up and make improvements."

When he's finished, we go back into the kitchen. The boss grabs a rag from the bucket brought in earlier and wipes down the table and the chairs. He and Mrs. Thomas sit across from each other. Molly stands off to the side, shifting her feet nervously. Tanya pets the kitten. The girls watch Mrs. Thomas and the boss with the concentration they usually give to their phones or computers.

Mrs. Thomas pulls out some papers, handing a set to the boss.

He flips through the pages. "This looks the same as the copy you emailed me." He's smiling, but I can smell his tension.

Mrs. Thomas studies him for a minute, fingering the papers in front of her. "Yes, but I'm afraid I'm going to have to change the rent." She reaches over and takes his set of papers.

Molly's hand tightens on the leash and Tanya sucks in her breath.

The boss's shoulders go rigid and his face pales. "I can't afford much more. I thought we'd agreed..." His voice is suddenly stringy.

Tanya's phone beeps. She pulls it from her pocket, sliding the kitten to one arm to do so. She stares at the screen a second and then shoves it back into her pants.

Molly gives her a quizzical look.

"Mama," Tanya mouths before returning her attention to the table.

Mrs. Thomas smiles. "We did." She studies him a moment more. "But as a good Christian—or I should say as someone trying to be a good Christian—I think if you're going to do all these repairs, I have to adjust the rent." She pauses. "A hundred dollars a month less. I'll still pay for the materials you need if you clear it with me beforehand."

For a moment, the boss stares at her without speaking. Then his shoulders relax. "That's . . . that would be wonderful!"

Mrs. Thomas picks up a pen and scratches something on each set of papers, and then she hands them to the boss, who writes on them.

Now the boss is all smiles. "Thank you," he says. "*Thank* you!" He pulls out his checkbook, writes on it, tears out the check and slides it over to her. Never understood checks except they seem important and the boss uses them to pay bills.

Then he offers his hand again. Not sure why because I thought all this hand shaking stuff was the human equivalent of dogs sniffing each other when they first meet. "You won't regret it. And . . ." His voice fades.

Mrs. Thomas's eyebrows raise. "What?"

"Well, if you ever decide to sell this place—not sure we could afford it, but would you let us know before the realtors get involved? Let us see if we could work it out?"

Mrs. Thomas nods. "I'm not thinking about that now, but if that happens, I'll definitely let you know."

Molly's grip on the leash relaxes and Tanya whispers, "Whew! Like watching a TV show." In a normal tone she says, "That was Mama. I gotta go." She strokes the kitten's head. "What should I do with Ms. Cutie here?"

Molly frowns, then turns to the boss. "Dad, could we put the kitten in Doodle's crate? Just till we go? It'll be cool enough with all the shade."

"Sure," the boss says. "Good idea." Still grinning, he looks as happy as a pup with a bowl of food.

We go out to the van and Molly opens the sliding door and then the gate to my crate. "You put her in, and I'll shut it super-fast," she says.

I'm not happy about having kitten scent all over my crate. Talk about air pollution, something the boss is always going on about. But no one asks me. I watch while Tanya peels the kitten's claws from her T-shirt, shoves her inside, and Molly slams the gate shut.

The kitten begins to yowl.

Tanya says goodbye and takes off down the sidewalk at a jog.

"I think I'll get her some water," Molly says.

Good idea. I'm a little thirsty myself.

She opens the back end of the van, takes my water bowl, and fills it from the jug of water the boss keeps for me.

But what the heck? She doesn't give it to me. She slips the gate open and shoves the bowl into it, spilling some in her hurry to shut the gate.

My crate. My water. I'm not happy about this at all! And the kitten doesn't even take a drink, but just keeps yowling. She's so loud I don't hear the sound of a car until it's pulling into the driveway. Startled, I give a single bark.

"Doodle!" Molly says, automatically.

The car is wide and sleek, but not new. Bits of rust show around the wheel rims and along the bottom edge. A sign with printing is attached to the side of the car. With a little whine, the driver's window goes down. A man older than the boss, his hair starting to show a little gray, smiles at us. He pats his forehead with a handkerchief and leans out the window.

"Hi, there." He eyes me nervously. "He bite?"

Molly laughs. "He's friendly. He's a bed bug dog. Well trained."

The man looks alarmed. "Bed bugs? Is he here because—"

"No," Molly shakes her head, still smiling. "We're renting the place."

"Really?" the man asks sharply. This seems to alarm him even more. He gets out, watching me with a caution that reminds me of the kitten. He's a stocky man with a paunch that spills over his belt. He's wearing slacks and what the boss calls a polo shirt, the kind that looks like a T-shirt with a collar. He smells like the stuff my second boss (don't get me started) used to splash on his face. Not fond of that scent.

"They inside?" he asks.

"Yeah," Molly answers.

He walks briskly to the door and disappears through it.

We follow him into the kitchen, where the boss and Mrs. Thomas are laughing about something.

Mrs. Thomas looks up and stares. "Denzel," she says in surprise.

"Mama, what's going on?" he asks, sounding irritated. "I've been trying to get hold of you. Your neighbor said you'd come over here. And—" he waves a pudgy hand at us "—they're saying something about being *renters*?" He gives her an accusing look.

Mrs. Thomas smiles and says, "I just leased this place to this fine man here." She turns to the boss. "Mr. Hunter, this is my son Denzel. He's with Assurance Realty. Denzel, this is Mr. Hunter. He runs a bed bug detection business."

"Call me Josh," the boss says. He rises, smiling, and extends a hand to Denzel.

But Denzel, his eyes on Mrs. Thomas, ignores the hand. "I thought I was going to manage this place. We talked about it. And I have several people interested. People I *told* that this house was available."

Mrs. Thomas sighs, and somehow looks a little sad. "*You* talked about it, yes. But Lamar—he's a friend from church—told me he knew of a good family looking for a place to live. I trust Lamar's judgment. And Mr. Hunter is willing to do some fixing up, which this place really needs."

Denzel pulls out his handkerchief and presses it to his forehead. "Mama, you really ought to leave this to me. It's my business, you know? We don't need to fix this up. Rentals are hot in Arlington right now. People will take anything they can find and pay premium rents." He pauses and says, "And sales are even hotter. It would be a great time to get your money out of this place."

"I've already told you I don't want to sell." There's an edge to her voice and her expression darkens.

Denzel raises his hands. "I know. I know. I'm just saying it's a hot market and it won't stay that way forever." He glances at the boss. "How much are they paying? I have people willing to pay $2,600 a month, as is—no repairs." He turns and glares at me. "Are they going to have this dog?"

"Two dogs," Mrs. Thomas says, suddenly cheerful. With a wink at Molly, she adds, "and probably a cat."

Molly beams back at her.

"Pets?" Denzel wails. "I *told* you pets can ruin a property. This is exactly why you should let me manage things. My prospects have no pets." He scowls and glares at the boss again. "How much are you paying?"

The boss starts to open his mouth, but Mrs. Thomas says firmly, "That is between Mr. Hunter and myself."

Denzel shakes his head, incredulous. "Do you *want* to lose money?"

"I want the right price for the right renter and I believe I got it."

"Unbelievable! Mama, why are you doing this? At your age you should be sitting back and enjoying life and leaving all this business stuff to others."

Mrs. Thomas's eyes flash. "*At my age*," she says, steel in her voice, "I have the experience to know what I want and how to get it. I don't need my child to tell me."

Silence.

"You say that," Denzel finally sputters, "but the smart thing is to use professionals for your business. If you needed surgery would you try to do it yourself? I've been in real estate for over ten years now and I know what to watch out for, things you need to have in the contract."

Mrs. Thomas stares at him, tight-lipped. She starts to speak, but then clamps her mouth shut.

"I mean, did you even get a contract?"

Whoa. The boss is clenching his fists, his shoulders tight again, all sorts of scents flooding from him. Anger. Tension.

"We have a contract," Mrs. Thomas says.

"For how long? Did you put in the terms you need to be able to evict them if they default on the rent or trash the place?" He gives the boss a hostile look. "People can say all sorts of things before they move in and then be totally different. And *pets*!"

"Denzel Raymond Thomas." Mrs. Thomas's voice rings out like that judge on the TV show Molly sometimes watches. "Enough! I've made my decision and signed a contract, and it's over. Now *you* need to get over it and go find those clients of yours somewhere else to rent." She's silent for a moment and then a bit of a smile, mostly in her eyes, softens her face. "I bet Mr. Hunter here knows of one that's going to be vacant in just a few weeks."

The boss's shoulders relax and he takes a deep breath. "As a matter of fact, I do," he says with a sidelong glance at Mrs. Thomas.

"Mama, you're just being stubborn like always. All right. You dug your grave. You can lie in it."

What? Graves? In the house?

Without another word, Denzel turns and stomps out, banging the screen door behind him.

No one speaks. Denzel's car engine starts, the brakes squealing as he backs out of the driveway. When the sound of the car has faded, the boss, his voice strained, says, "Listen. I really would like to live here, but if it's going to cause family problems. . ."

Mrs. Thomas sighs. "I'm sorry you had to hear that. That boy would run my life if he could." Her mouth twists. "Especially if money is involved."

The boss says, "As long as you're okay with it. With us. I won't hold you to the contract if you want to change your mind."

Mrs. Thomas gives him a bright smile. "And that's why I know you're going to a great renter! I told you I trust Lamar's judgement and I do, and you've just proven you're an honest man." She reaches into her briefcase and pulls out a set of keys. "I believe you'll need these. They work for both the front and back door. You can make copies if you need. Rent is due on the first, but you can start moving in and doing repairs right away if you'd like." She zips shut her briefcase and rises.

The boss takes the keys, a grin plastered on his face. "Thank you. *Thank* you! I'll do right by you, I promise."

She gives him an appraising look. "I do believe you will!"

We all walk her out to her car and watch as she drives away.

And then the boss takes Molly's arms and swings her around in that kind of dance thing they do when they're really happy.

"We got it! We got it!" He laughs.

"Oh, Dad," Molly giggles, plainly delighted.

I try to join in, but Molly still laughing says, "Doodle, off!"

The boss pulls Molly to him, gives her a kiss on the cheek and lets her go.

"Got to tell Annie," he says, pulling out his phone. And then, as if he's just won the lottery, which he always says is a *really* big deal, "We got the house!"

Chapter 3

Moving In

Today is our last day at the old house. Good thing, too, because all the back and forth of moving everything to the new place has made the boss and Molly grumpy. I'm exhausted just watching them.

So. Much. Stuff. Every bit has to be loaded into the van or Annie's truck and carted over to the new place and then unloaded. Again and again. Van load after van load. Truck load after truck load.

Not my stuff, of course. My bed, dishes, harnesses, and collars fit in the van with room to spare. Dogs don't collect stuff like people do.

And then there is the cleaning. Everything has to be wiped down in both the old house and the new one. The oven cleaned—what a horrible stench!—the fridge wiped out and all the floors vacuumed or swept and mopped. The boss says we have to leave the old house spotless so he'll get his deposit back.

I spend a lot of time in the backyard of the old place so I won't, in the words of the boss, "get in the way." Not my favorite place to be so I'm glad when Molly finally brings me back inside.

"That's it!" the boss says, his grumpiness gone. He beams at me and Molly. "It's finally happening!"

Molly is all smiles, too, as we walk through every room, the boss regarding each space with a critical eye. He takes photos with his phone. "Just in case the landlord tries to be a jerk about the deposit," he says. Not sure what he means, but every room is checked and photographed and then we go out to the backyard.

The boss and Molly are always good about keeping my poop cleaned up, but we march around the yard one more time to make sure they didn't miss any. Of course, any new dog who comes to this place will still find my scent. But humans, with their inferior sense of smell, will never know.

At last, Molly loads me into my crate, gets into the van, which for once isn't crowded with stuff, and we drive to the new house.

"Annie will be here this afternoon," the boss says as we're walking through the front door. "As soon as she gets off work."

His phone buzzes. He stares at the screen a second, then swipes it. "Hunter Bed Bug Detection," he says in the voice he uses for business. But then his face moves into a smile "Oh, hi. I didn't recognize your number." He listens for a second. "Sure. I'll come right over."

He pockets his phone. "They got the AC window units in. Didn't expect them until Friday."

He turns to Molly. "Want a break from unpacking?"

She nods emphatically. "Yes! For about two years."

He smiles, but then the smile fades as he looks down at me. "Too hot to take Doodle." He rubs his beard. "I think he'll be fine in the backyard. I left him there all afternoon the other day when Lamar and I were doing the tile."

"He can hang out with Moxy," Molly says, "if she isn't too scared to come out of the mudroom."

Moxy is the kitten. Molly named her that because she thinks the kitten is gutsy. I don't know about that. If gutsy means yowling your head off whenever you want something, then I suppose the kitten qualifies. It has no relation, if you were wondering, to the kind of guts a dog might eat if he happens to catch a rabbit.

Moxy has lived here since the day we found her. After a lot of discussion between the boss, Molly, and Annie, as well as a phone call to Mrs. Thomas, it was decided to keep the kitten at the new place. According to Annie, cats get anxious when they are in a new environment. She thought it would be hard on the kitten to take her to our old place for only a few weeks. (Just another way dogs are superior to cats. Dogs don't care where they are as much as who they are with. But cats have always been all about themselves.)

Annie came up with the solution. Keep the kitten at the new place, in the mudroom with a litter box at night, and install a cat door so she can go outside when she wants during the daytime.

Oh, the litter box! How is it that I've never encountered one before? What a deliciously fragrant thing that is after the kitten has used it a time or two! Sadly, everyone gets instantly angry if I so much as lower my nose in its direction. No idea why. They spend all sorts of time cleaning it out and I could save them the trouble. Just sayin'...

Anyway, we've been coming over every day since the boss met with Mrs. Thomas, so Moxy isn't as afraid of me as she first was. She can still get huffy if I get too close, though.

Molly takes me through the mudroom past the forbidden litterbox to the backyard. Moxy is sleeping in her favorite spot, a high shelf opposite the washer and dryer, and doesn't so much as blink an eye when we walk by.

Pausing to stroke me under my chin for a second, Molly says, "You be a good dog. We'll be back soon."

I find a cool spot on the grass under one of the big trees and settle down for a nap. Have to say I love this yard.

I'm just starting to doze when Moxy pokes her head through the cat door, and then cautiously comes out into the yard. Tail straight up, back hunched, she creeps toward me, ready to bolt if I make a move. Silly cat. I lie there and watch her.

When I raise my head, the kitten shies, but then, after a moment of watching me intensely, she creeps closer. Cats are not the bravest of creatures. They're even more skittish than horses, although fortunately not as big. I wait, holding still, until the kitten is close enough that I could grab it with a single lunge forward. I don't, of course. I keep still. And finally, Moxy bumps my nose with hers, then jumps back, watching me warily. I don't move. She bumps it again, and we sniff each other briefly and she jumps back again. This repeats several times until she finally relaxes and, allowing me to sniff her butt, she starts purring and rubs against my chest.

This is the closest I've ever been to a cat except Miga, Molly's mother's cat. I'm not a big fan of cats as you might have gathered, but this one evidently is going to be part of our family, so we need to be on good terms. And I'll have to admit that it's nice having company in the backyard. Dogs really aren't meant to be alone. It's not in our nature.

After a while, Moxy curls up against my side and goes to sleep. It's pleasant out here under the big trees with her by my side. I doze off.

I awake to barking. A dog running down the street. In a flash, Moxy shoots across the yard and through the cat door. But the dog—hey, I recognize that bark! Cooper! Cooper keeps going, past our house, down the street.

I rush over to the fence but can't see much through the skinny spaces between the boards.

As Cooper's barking fades, another sound replaces it. Footsteps of someone running.

"Cooper!" comes a voice. It's that boy, Cooper's owner. "Cooooooper! Come!"

Lots of tension in that voice, not to mention anger. "Coooper!"

I hate to tell this boy, but Cooper is long gone. And even if he weren't, he probably wouldn't want to come, not when the boy is so upset.

But then the footsteps stop. I hear the boy breathing hard, noisy gasps. "What am I going to do?" he cries, in between the gasps. And then, a small moan. "Oh, no. Oh, no. Not this!"

There is a thud. A brief silence. And then, almost too soft to hear, "Help. Help."

Something is seriously wrong. I let out a volley of barks, but when they fade, I hear nothing, not even the boy's breathing. And even though I'm not the service dog type, I know this boy needs help. And I have to try.

I bark again, hoping to alert someone. No response.

This fence is taller than the one in the old place. I get a running start and push off with all my strength, hoping to get high enough to scrabble over. Instead, I hit hard against the boards and fall back. I try again. No luck and it hurts to hit the wood like that. I try again and again. Sore, tired, I'm about to give up when I hear the boy moan again. I try a different section of the fence, push off and once again hit it hard. But this time, the old boards give way, creaking forward and I'm just able to claw my way over.

The boy is lying half on the strip of grass and half on the sidewalk. I rush over to him, sniff him, lick his face. He's breathing, but he doesn't respond. I lick him again and bark in his face. No response. And he smells—well, I can't describe it except the normal "boy" scents are tainted with something that smells off. Somehow wrong. The boy needs help, no doubt about it.

I start barking like a maniac. I bark and bark and even howl a few times. Finally, a door opens in the house across the street and a woman sticks her head out. I leave the boy, running across the street to bark at her.

"What on earth?" She steps outside. She's a heavyset Latina wearing a housedress.

I race back to the boy and bark at her from there. Trying to get people—who are generally clueless—to understand what a dog wants is always hard and often impossible. But somehow, this woman gets the idea. She follows me across the street, takes one look at the boy, and gasps, "Jordan!" She sinks to her knees and pats his face. "Jordan, are you okay?"

Clearly not, and when he doesn't answer, she pulls out her phone. She waits while it rings. "Come on, Keira, answer!" she says.

"Hey, this is Keira," a voice says. "Leave a message at the tone."

The woman gives an explosive frustrated sound.

"Keira, this is Anita Olejandro from down the street. Jordan's passed out on the sidewalk. I'm calling 911."

She taps her phone a few times and then says, "I have an emergency. A neighbor's boy is unconscious on the sidewalk here. He's diabetic and I think he might be in a coma." She listens for a second. "Yes. He's breathing. But they're fast and shallow breaths," she says, the words tumbling out.

She rattles off numbers and a street name, telling the woman on the other end that no one else is around.

Then she pockets the phone. "They're sending EMTs," she says, looking down at me. "You're a good dog, aren't you." She reaches over to pet me, and I move closer, wagging my tail a little.

She strokes my fur, and we wait together for what seems a long time. Every so often she pulls out her phone and tries to call someone. Jordan doesn't wake up, doesn't change. He still has that odd smell.

At last, I hear sirens, and shortly after the woman says, "That's them!"

And then we see the flashing lights and an ambulance pulls up to the curb. A man and a woman jump out and hurry over to Jordan.

They talk in low voices, saying phrases I don't understand. And then something else takes my attention: I see our van coming down the road.

The boss pulls into the driveway, hops out of the car, and runs over to the EMTs. "What's going on?"

Molly, right behind him, comes to me. "Doodle," she says taking my collar. Her tension flows through her hand.

"This is your dog?" the neighbor woman asks.

Molly nods. "Did he . . . did he cause a problem?" Her eyes are wide, fearful.

"Problem? No. He probably saved Jordan's life. He kept barking, wouldn't stop, you know? So I went out to see what the matter was. And when I opened my door, he ran over to me, barked some more and then ran back here." The woman shakes her head, her voice suddenly thickening. "If he hadn't barked like that . . ."

Molly's grip on my collar relaxes. "*Good* boy, Doodle," she says. She looks over to where the EMTs are loading Jordan onto a stretcher. "*Good* boy."

When at last the EMT vehicle drives away, lights flashing, everything seems suddenly quiet. After a moment, the neighbor goes over to the boss. "I'm Anita Olejandro," she says. "I'm across the street, one house down. And I guess you're the new people moving into the Thomas place."

The boss nods, smiling. "Josh Hunter," he says, "and this is my daughter, Molly."

"And Doodle," Molly says, always the one to remember me.

"Doodle, is it?" Anita asks. "He's a hero. Should be on YouTube."

The boss gives her a blank look.

Anita explains how my barking got her to open her door. "I think poor Jordan might have died right there on the sidewalk if Doodle here hadn't barked like that."

The boss reaches out a hand and touches me softly on the head. He glances back at the fence, which has a definite sag where I went over it. "I thought he wouldn't be able to climb this one." He shakes his head.

"Good thing he could!" Anita answers.

A sedan speeding down the road brakes suddenly, and pulls up to the curb.

"Keira!" Anita says. She turns to us and in a lower voice adds, "Jordan's mother."

The window of the car comes down and a woman sticks her head out. She's thin and dressed like people do for work—a shiny blouse, makeup, small earrings. "Where's is he?" she asks, her eyes wide, her voice harsh with fear. "Where's Jordan?"

Anita hurries over to the car. "At Madison General," she says. "They said he'll be okay. Wouldn't have been except for this dog here."

"Dog?" Keira blinks, looking confused.

"Doodle here," Anita says. "Tried to alert the whole neighborhood."

"*Alert?*" Keira glances around wildly, turning her head in every direction. And then, "Where's Cooper?"

Chapter 4

Searching

"Where's Cooper?" Keira asks again, her voice high and distressed. "He was supposed to keep this from happening! That . . . *dog*." Now her voice changes to anger. "Hasn't been right since we got him. Pulls on the leash. Pees in the house, but I thought that's okay as long as he does what he's supposed to do—keep—" she waves an arm at the sidewalk "—keep this from happening." She starts to cry. "All that money, all that help from everyone, and now this?"

Anita says, in a calm low voice, "It'll be okay. Let's get you to the hospital. I don't think you should drive. If you'll let me take you there, I can get my daughter to pick me up." She opens the door to the car and takes Keira's arm. "Let's just get you to the other side here, and we'll have you with Jordan in no time."

Still crying, Keira gets out of the car and allows Anita to lead her around to the passenger side. "But Cooper . . ."

"We'll find him," Molly says. "We'll go right now and search."

The boss adds, in his everyone-keep-calm voice, "Like Molly said, we'll find him. We'll get a search party out. You go to your son. We'll worry about Cooper."

"He's just not *right,* you know? He's not what we thought a service dog would be?" She swipes her eyes and takes a long, shuddering breath, then sinks into the passenger seat.

"Wait," the boss says. He digs in his pocket and pulls out his wallet, and then thrusts one of his business cards through the window. "My phone's on this. If you send me a text after things have settled down, I can let you know when we find Cooper."

Keira takes the card without a word, and then the car pulls away and is gone.

Molly instantly pulls out her phone. "Tanya," she says. Talking very fast, she explains the situation.

The boss is on his phone as well. "Just letting Annie know," he says.

The boss lets Annie know about everything. He texts her almost more often than Molly does Tanya, which, believe me, is a lot.

Before long, the Franklins' van drives up. Mrs. Franklin and Tanya get out.

"Barbara," the boss says with a warm smile when Mrs. Franklin goes over to him. "Thanks so much for coming." If, as the boss says, Mr. Franklin and the boys are built like telephone poles, Mrs. Franklin is more like a pillow with legs. A firm pillow. Almost as tall as her husband, she's much broader. I don't know if I've mentioned she's one of my favorite people. She calls me her substitute dog and always gives me extra leftovers.

"Sorry it's just Tanya and me. Lamar and Derrin are at work," Mrs. Franklin says. "Kenny's at a practice, and Tyson is mowing a neighbor's lawn. Any idea which way he went?"

The boss shakes his head. "He could be anywhere."

I know exactly which way he went, but good luck letting everyone know that. But by the way Cooper was running, the boss is right. By now, he could be anywhere.

"He could be back home by now," Molly says.

They talk about it for a few minutes and decide that the boss and Mrs. Franklin will each search from their vans, while Molly and Tanya walk over to Jordan's house and search that area. The boss gives Molly and Mrs. Franklin an extra leash in case they find Cooper.

I go with Molly, of course. We set off down the road.

"Coooooper!" Molly calls. Tanya echoes that.

"It's just a block and a half down the road," Tanya announces, in between calling for Cooper.

"You've been there before?" asks Molly.

"Yeah. We helped put up the backyard fence." She wipes her face. "Hot today."

"I know," Molly answers. "That's why we had to leave Doodle when Dad and I went to town. Good thing, too." She explains how I barked and jumped over the fence.

"Bet your dad won't be happy about that!" Tanya exclaims.

"I know!" Molly agrees fervently. "But he didn't actually seem too upset. I mean, Doodle might have saved Jordan's life."

We cross a side street, the girls calling for Cooper constantly, and then Tanya points at an older brick home with a recently mowed lawn and small porch. "That's it there."

The strip of lawn in front is as skinny as the one at our place, but it's all grass rather than weeds. Lots of cat scents, of course. Like I said, cats are everywhere. Next to the house is a garden with tall fragrant flowers. The backyard has a chain-link fence, the kind with the slats in it so you can't easily see through it.

"Coooooper!" Molly calls. She leads me over to the fence, which isn't as tall as ours, and peers into the backyard. "Not here," she says. I could have told her that by the staleness of his scent.

"Our family helped put this up," Tanya tells Molly. "You have to have a fenced yard to qualify to get a service dog, so Mrs. Taylor bought the materials and a bunch of people from the church installed it."

"That's why it looks so new." Molly gives it an appraising glance. "Much newer than the one we have."

We leave the yard and move on down the street, Tanya telling Molly about the Taylors in between shouting out Cooper's name.

"Jordan's dad was killed in Afghanistan," Tanya says. "He was in the army. Jordan was only seven when his dad died."

There is a moment of silence, both girls looking sad.

"That'd be tough," Molly says at last.

Tanya agrees, and then shouts out, "Coooooper!"

We walk for some time, each girl checking her phone every so often in case the boss or Mrs. Franklin found the dog. At one point, Molly announces, "Jordan's okay. Mrs. Taylor texted Dad. They'll be coming home soon." She sighs, shaking her head. "Wish we'd found Cooper."

"Yeah," Tanya agrees.

But when we finally give up and head for home, we find Cooper back at his house, lying on the porch, panting hard, tongue drooping, a happy, goofy expression on his face. His leash hangs down from his collar.

"I better get him," Tanya says. "In case Doodle makes him nervous."

Molly agrees and we hang back while Tanya marches up the steps of the porch and takes the leash. "Cooper!" she says. "You've been a very bad dog." But her voice is friendly. Cooper licks her hand and keeps panting.

"I don't think he's a bit sorry either" Molly says.

I have to agree. Cooper looks like he had a great time. There is joy in running full out, going where your nose takes you, stopping to sniff wherever you want, not having to listen to instructions from anyone. The joy of complete freedom. Something I don't think humans understand.

Molly and Tanya both pull out their phones, evidently texting. Predictably, a few seconds later, their phones beep.

"Mama says Mrs. Taylor is on her way home with Jordan," Tanya says, her eyes on her phone. "His blood sugar crashed really low and they had to get it back to normal, but now he's fine. She told us to wait with Cooper until they get here."

Tanya sits down on the porch beside Cooper, and Molly and I sit on the bottom step. We wait for what seems like a long time before I hear Mrs. Taylor's car down the road.

"Cooper!" Jordan exclaims as he gets out of the car. His voice is a mixture of relief and anger.

Cooper jumps up and tugs at the leash, pulling Tanya over to meet Jordan.

"He yanked it right out of my hand," Jordan says, taking the leash. "And just took off down the road. I ran after him and tried to catch him, but then . . . well, you know."

Keira, carrying a white plastic bag along with a purse, joins us. Her eyes are red and her face sags with exhaustion. "You girls are wonderful! I don't know how to thank you!"

"We didn't do anything," Molly insists, "except look for him. He was here when we got back."

Jordan bends down to pat Cooper on the head. "At least he knows his way home. That's good, right?"

"It's something, I guess," Keira says, her voice grim. "But it's not what we paid for. What—" she waves an arm at Tanya "—all of you helped pay for. Service dogs aren't supposed to run off."

No kidding.

"Who'd you get him from?" Molly asks.

"Life Support Service Canines," Keira answers.

"Annie—she's the one my dad's marrying—trains dogs. She works with a great trainer, Miguel De Castillo, who trains all kinds of scent detection dogs—bed bug, mold, termites. Maybe she could help."

Keira sighs. "We've had so much help, you know?" Her mouth forms a thin hard line. "The person who needs to help is Mr. Banes. Since we started having problems with Cooper, I've been doing some research. Which I should have done more of in the first place. No service dog should pull like Cooper and run away. He needs more training. I'm going to call Mr. Banes and tell him we want another dog. He has a guarantee. I think a trip to the emergency room is evidence that Cooper's not up to the job."

At this, Jordan sucks in his breath. "But I like Cooper," he says, patting the still panting Cooper on the head.

"We don't have him for you to like," Keira snaps. "We have him to save your life, which he didn't do." She tilts her head toward me. "It took a dog who doesn't even know you to get help while Cooper was cruising the neighborhood."

Whoa. She's angry. Jordan's eyes narrow and he stares at his feet.

"He said we needed to give Cooper time," Jordan mumbles to the sidewalk. "To settle in. He hasn't had a fair trial."

"He's had over a month. Most service dogs settle in right away."

"But I *like* him." Jordan's eyes are still on his toes.

"That doesn't matter! He's not a *pet*. He's a dog who's supposed to keep you alive."

Molly suddenly strokes my neck. The boss is always telling her I'm not a pet. Which is actually a good thing. I like having a job. I think most dogs do.

"And if Mr. Banes doesn't make this good, I'm going to sue his—" Kiera glances at Molly and Tanya "—his pants off. If he thinks I'm some poor widow he can cheat, he'll find out he's wrong."

Whoa. Her voice is hard enough that the hair on my back starts to rise.

While she's talking, the Franklins' van pulls up to the curb. Mrs. Franklin gets out and comes over. She hands my extra leash to Molly and then turns to Keira.

"You must have been scared out of your mind." She opens her arms and after a slight hesitation, Keira moves into them for a long hug.

"Thanks," she says, swiping at her eyes as she steps back.

"You need *anything*, you let us know, girl. Okay?" Mrs. Franklin says.

Keira nods, her eyes welling again.

Mrs. Franklin turns to Tanya. "We need to get home or I'll be late for work."

"Thanks again," Keira calls out as Tanya and Mrs. Franklin hurry toward the van.

The boss shows up just as they pull away. He walks up to us, gives Kiera a big smile and, with a glance at Cooper, says, "The prodigal returns home!"

Not sure what he means, but Keira's mouth twists into a grimace. Her eyes are still angry.

"I'm Josh Hunter," the boss says. "Molly's dad. I don't know if you heard, but we've just moved into the Thomas place."

Keira nods, but her eyes are still on Cooper.

The boss turns to Jordan. "You're doing okay now?"

"Yeah, fine," Jordan mumbles, head still down.

No one speaks for a moment, and then the boss says to Molly, "We better be getting back. Solid boxes in the living room," he says with another smile at Keira. She nods but doesn't smile back.

But when she thanks the boss again, her eyes soften. "Really appreciate it. You have a great dog there."

The boss looks surprised. No idea why. "He has his moments," he says.

Molly loads me into my crate, and we drive back to our place.

"She's got her hands full," the boss says after we're inside. "Service dog my foot!"

I glance at his feet, not quite understanding.

"I know." Molly tells him what Keira said about demanding a replacement. "She said the company had a guarantee."

"Well, that's good then." The boss is studying the label on a box. "Found the silverware!" He lifts the box and carries it to kitchen, setting it on the counter. "One down, only about two million to go."

"Jordan's not happy about it," Molly says. "He likes Cooper."

The boss looks up from the box and meets Molly's eyes. "That boy could have died. Cooper's supposed to be a working dog, not a pet. Just like Doodle."

See what I mean? I bet he could give the "Doodle's not a pet" speech in his sleep.

But Molly bends down and strokes me under my chin, which I love. "Yeah," she says, "but sometimes some dogs can be both."

Chapter 5

Settling In

When we get home, Molly and the boss spend a lot of time opening boxes and putting things away. I nap, as there's nothing I can contribute to this. I'd prefer to nap on my bed, the soft one that was in the living room at the old house, but it's leaning upright against the wall because boxes are taking up all the floor space.

I'd just as soon be in the backyard, under the big tree, but when I stand at the back door, my signal to the boss to let me out, he just looks at me and says, "Not on your life. Not till I get that fence fixed."

So I find a quiet corner in Molly's room, which so far only has her bed, desk, and computer unpacked. I look for the rug I usually sleep on, but it isn't here either, so I curl down on the wood floor.

After a series of naps, I hear Annie's truck. Annie has been our good friend ever since we met her when the boss and I were practicing for my bed bug certification test. Since then, she and the boss have become even better friends and now are going to get married. Then she and Chloe will move in with us.

Annie comes in smelling of enchiladas, a favorite of mine, but she's carrying a box that smells like paper.

"We got almost all the kitchen put away," Molly announces.

Annie is one of those people whose smile makes you feel happy just to be around her. She gives this smile now, and the boss and Molly grin back at her. Almost as tall as the boss, she has light, shoulder-length hair that she wears pulled back with an elastic band. She's dressed in jeans and a long-sleeved cotton shirt, her usual outfit.

Molly and the boss help Annie bring in more boxes and then, finally, the pan of enchiladas that I've been smelling.

"Compliments of Miguel," she says, her expression oddly smug.

"Miguel made these?" the boss asks surprised. Miguel is my trainer and Annie's boss. He's great with dogs, but not so much in the kitchen, at least when I lived there.

Annie smiles. "Not exactly. Miguel heated them up. They were actually made by Rosa Mirandez." She says the name slowly as if it's important. "Who has been spending a lot of time at Miguel's."

The boss raises his eyebrows. "Miguel has a girlfriend?" He looks astonished.

Annie nods triumphantly. "Yes! And I like her a lot. She's sweet but no pushover if you know what I mean. Doesn't take any guff."

I'm not sure at all what she means, but the boss nods. "That's wonderful! Amazing, really. He's no spring chicken."

Now I'm really confused. Miguel doesn't even have chickens, which in my opinion is a smart move.

"Love isn't just for the young!" Annie says, with a fond glance at the boss.

Annie places the enchiladas on the table along with a salad she brought. Molly puts out silverware and plates, and the boss gets the glasses and drinks.

When they're all seated, the boss raises his glass of diet ginger ale and says, "To us!" Annie raises her glass of Diet Coke and Molly her Pepsi, and they all clink them together.

Why the boss loves diet ginger ale, which smells like some kind of cleaning chemical, is beyond me, but he does. He's said several times that beer used to be his favorite drink until it "became a problem" after he and Molly's mother split up years ago. That's when he switched to ginger ale. Beer smells and tastes just as bad or worse than diet ginger ale, so no loss there. Of course, Diet Coke is no better. Maybe if humans had a better sense of smell, they'd stick to good drinks like milk and water.

"I'm going to bring one of Chloe's crates over tomorrow," Annie says, "and bring Chloe for a little bit so she can get used to the house and meet Moxy before we're here all the time."

At this, the boss takes her hand. "Only two and half more weeks," he says, radiating happiness.

Molly suddenly sets down her fork, and with this I-have-a-bright-idea look on her face says, "You know what would be cool? If I walked Doodle down the aisle and he had the rings on his collar or something."

Annie laughs. "That could be fun."

But the boss, with more of an are-you-kidding-me expression, says, "I don't think so. Just asking for trouble."

"Doodle's part of our family," Molly protests. "Just like you and me. Don't you think he should be at the wedding? And he's trained to be good in public places."

The boss frowns, clearly not happy with the idea.

But Annie says, "We could do it! Add a little spice to the ceremony." She grins at Molly.

"By spice do you mean disaster?" But then the boss meets Annie's eyes and the lines in his face relax. "Maybe, I guess."

Molly squints in the way she does when thinking. Then, to Annie, "But Chloe's part of your family, too. So we need both dogs. And then we'll have *all* the family at the wedding."

Now the boss looks positively alarmed. "It'd be too much to walk two dogs in a strange place. Truly begging for trouble."

"What about Tanya?" Molly asks. "She could walk Chloe beside me and Doodle. She's practically part of our family and she'll be there anyway to sing." Molly, her eyes anxious, searches Annie's face. "Unless you have someone from your side of the family you'd like to walk Chloe?"

"This is getting awfully complicated," the boss says. "What if Doodle barks or Chloe howls? Or one of them has, um, an accident?"

An accident? Seriously? What if I suddenly sprouted wings and flew up to the rooftop?

But Annie reaches out and puts her hand on Molly's arm. "Brilliant idea! That'd be perfect. None of my family will be here soon enough to practice, but we can run through it with you girls and the dogs in advance—" she turns to smile at the boss "—so we know there won't be any problems. And, if something unexpected happens, we'll laugh and remind ourselves it's not the wedding that's important, it's the marriage."

She brushes the boss's cheek with her hand, and his eyes go soft and a little spacey like they do when she touches him.

"Okay," he sighs. And then, maybe only half-kidding, "I can see that I'll need to be careful that the women in this family don't gang up against the only man."

Molly and Annie grin at each other.

With that, they all go back to eating until the boss says abruptly, "I've got to look at that fence!"

"I thought that was done," Annie says.

"It was." The boss gives me a glance, his expression not entirely happy.

"Doodle saved a boy's life," Molly says. She tells Annie about Jordan collapsing and how I barked until someone came out to see what was wrong."

"Barked *outside* the fence," the boss interjects.

"He got through it?" Now it's Annie's turn to look surprised.

"Only, I think, because the boards are old in one section and they gave way. I thought the support I put up there was enough, but evidently not. I'll probably have to buy a few boards." He sighs and then says, "I'll tell you one thing. That dog of Jordan's is no service dog. He's hardly trained at all. Compared to him, Doodle's the best trained dog in the world."

Molly says, "But Cooper is nice. He's not aggressive or anything, just . . ."

"Wild," the boss says.

Annie frowns. "And he's supposed to be a service dog?"

"I know," Molly says. "Doesn't act like one at all." She turns to Annie. "Maybe you could help him—Jordan. Show him how to control Cooper."

Annie shakes her head vigorously. "They should take him back to the kennel. That's who's responsible." She sighs. "And I have approximately a million and two things to do before the wedding."

Molly bites her lip but doesn't say anything.

After dishes are done, she takes me out back to pee. Moxy watches us go through the mud room with interest but not alarm, and then follows us outside.

"Aren't you a brave kitty!" Molly says in that high tone people sometimes use with animals. Moxy goes over to her and weaves in and out of her legs.

What? I finish peeing and zoom back to Molly. Moxy darts away when I come running, and I start to follow her, but Molly commands "NO!" in a loud voice. "No chase!" She gives me a stern look. I go back to lean against her for a moment and then return to sniffing the yard.

She takes out her phone. I hear ringing and then Tanya's voice.

"Guess what?" Molly doesn't wait for an answer. "How would you like to be part of the wedding?"

"I'm doing a solo, right?" Tanya says.

"How would you like to do more?" She explains about walking me and Chloe down the aisle.

"What if I can't control her?" Tanya asks, her voice uncertain.

"We'll practice," Molly assures her. "If it doesn't work, we don't have to do it."

She and Molly talk some more. They never seem to run out of things to say to each other.

I trot off to investigate some interesting scents along the fence on the opposite side of the driveway. When I hear Molly say goodbye to Tanya, I look up to see Moxy rubbing against her legs again. Hey! I hurry over to make sure Molly remembers me. This time, Moxy only jumps back a little, and then—what the? —she starts to rub against my legs.

"Well, look at you two," Molly says. "Already best friends."

Hardly how I'd put it! I'm glad when we go back inside and the kitten has to stay in the mudroom.

Moxy's not glad, though. She meows at the door with a plaintive, forlorn sound that's plenty loud even in the living room where the boss and Annie are sitting on our couch, boxes surrounding them.

"Someone wants in," Annie says.

The boss shakes his head. "Someone needs to learn that she's not going to be a house cat," he replies in a stern voice.

Annie smiles cryptically and says, "We'll see."

"We won't see," the boss states with vehemence. "I don't want an indoor cat!"

After a bit, the boss sighs and gets to his feet. "Back to work. These boxes aren't going to unpack themselves." He's been saying that a lot lately even though I think that's pretty obvious. He selects a box and carries into the bathroom. Annie joins him, her arms full with another one, and soon they're talking about what should go where.

I doze in Molly's bedroom while she takes piles of her clothes from boxes and either hangs them up or puts them in drawers. This room is bigger than her old one, so she doesn't have to step over me to get to the closet. Still missing the rug, however.

It's getting to be about time for my bedtime pee, when Molly wakes me up. "Look what I found!" She's holding my rug. I rush over to sniff it, to see if it's still the same, which it is.

"Doodle, move," Molly says. "I can't put it down if you're in the way." She gently pushes me back and puts the rug down next to her bed.

Perfect. It's thick, what Molly calls plush, and it's much nicer to sleep on than the wood floor.

"See you tomorrow," Annie calls from the living room.

"Thank Miguel for the enchiladas," the boss says. "Or Rosa." He's smiling at Annie, but then his phone buzzes. He glances at it, frowns, and after a moment says, "Josh Hunter." He taps something on his phone and to Annie mouths, "Speaker."

Whoa. Suddenly the voice comes over the phone loud enough that everyone can hear it.

"Hi, Josh. Keira Taylor. I hope this isn't too late to call." Her voice is upset, angry even.

"No, not at all. What's up?"

She hesitates. "I'm calling because, well, you know about dogs and training, right? I've spent all evening trying to contact Kirby Banes, Cooper's trainer. His phone's been disconnected, and I tried email, but he doesn't answer. I finally went to the website to try to call LSSC and guess what?"

She now sounds angry enough that if it were me, I'd be hesitant to guess.

"It's not quite the same. It looks different. And I when I search Kirby Banes, the name doesn't come up at all."

Chapter 6

Spoofed!

It's muggy today and hot, even in the shade on the front porch, where Molly and I are waiting for Tanya. What I call panting weather. Inside the house is not much better. The boss has been working on installing the air conditioners. but from his grumbling I suspect it isn't going well. He says he needs some lumber for supports. "More money. Everything costs money," he laments. Which is pretty much his philosophy in a nutshell.

Molly's sitting on one of the plastic lawn chairs that the boss moved from our old backyard to the porch—much better than the ones that were here when we moved in. I'm at her feet.

The boss loves the porch. "Best feature of the house," he's said more than once. I'm partial to the backyard myself, since I always have to be on a leash out front.

Molly watches the street in the direction that Tanya comes from while I doze. But then she straightens up. "It's Jordan," she says, looking the opposite way.

I sit up. Sure enough, Jordan is striding quickly towards us. He doesn't have Cooper. He slows down when he comes to our yard and turns in.

"Hey," Molly says. She motions for him to join us, which he does. He sinks into a lawn chair, brushing the sweat off his forehead with his fingers. His eyes are red in the way of people who've been crying. He stares at his feet.

Molly, seeing his face, asks, "Are you okay?"

Jordan raises his head. "I . . .I need your help. Everything was a fake. All of it. Mama says we're the two stupidest people to ever get a dog."

"What? Fake?" Molly looks confused.

I see a motion down the street and sit up. Tanya's hurrying toward us.

Molly waves and soon Tanya comes up the steps. She's wearing sandals, shorts and a sleeveless blouse and has her hair in braids pinned to her head.

"Hey, Jordan," she says. "Hot enough." She plops down into a chair beside Molly. She smells like bacon and fresh mown grass. And sweat, of course.

Molly says, "Jordan was just about to tell us what happened with Cooper and his trainer.

Jordan hesitates for a moment, looking from Molly to Tanya. "You know how Mama couldn't get hold of the trainer last night?"

Tanya says, "Yeah. Molly told me your mama called last night."

"Well, today, when she got up, Mama was really mad. She decided we were going to take Cooper back to the kennel and demand that they give us a different dog." His eyes go back to his feet and he swallows hard. "Even though Cooper and I really get along, you know? Even if he doesn't always do what I ask."

"That would be hard." Molly's eyes are soft with sympathy. "But if they can retrain him, you'd still have him." I lie back down sniffing discreetly at Jordan's jeans and shoes. I'm happy to discover he doesn't have a cat.

Jordan nods. "That's what I said. Give Cooper a chance first. So we put Cooper in the car and drive to the place. It's out toward Manassas in the country, and it takes us awhile to find it."

"You'd never been there before?" Molly asks in surprise.

Jordan shakes his head. "The *trainer—*" he says the word like it's sour in his mouth "—always came to our place. He brought the application over himself, because he said if our home environment wasn't suitable, it would save us the application fee. Which sounded good, you know? It cost $25 to apply."

"Uh-oh," Tanya says.

"Yeah," Jordan says bitterly. "Anyway, we find the place, and it looks great. Trees, kennels. Clean looking. We see someone walking a dog, a yellow Lab like Cooper, out behind the office. So we go inside. Cooper gets all excited and starts rearing up and pulling against his harness like he does. I think maybe because he recognizes the place and is happy to be back.

"I try to hold him while Mama goes to the counter, slaps down all the paperwork we got from Mr. Banes and says to the receptionist, this thin man with an earring, 'You see how he behaves? You can't tell me he was properly trained. I need to speak to Mr. Banes. Or if he's not here, to whoever runs this place.'"

Jordan swallows again and wipes the sweat from his face.

"The man looks all flustered and tells Mama he's just a volunteer, but he'll call Lisa, the manager. Cooper keeps barking no matter how many times I tell him to hush.

"So pretty soon Lisa comes out, and she looks worried, you know? I'd kind of gotten Cooper to settle down, but when he sees her, he starts all over again, jumping up, barking. Lisa comes over to me and says, 'Do you mind?' She's carrying one of those thin rope leashes and slips it over his neck, and then works with him for a few minutes, and gets him calmed down. She's really good, and I can see Cooper likes her. And I'm thinking that maybe she'll tell Mama he just needs a little more training and he'll be perfect.

"Lisa says, 'a harness doesn't give you good control when a dog's acting out like this.'

"Mama says, 'You're telling me! This dog has had problems from day one and you need to do something about it.'

"Lisa's eyes go all sympathetic. 'We're not a general training facility here,' she says carefully, like maybe Mama's drunk or crazy. 'But I could give you names of reputable trainers if you'd like.'

"And Mama about goes ballistic and says, 'That's your job. I paid all that money for a dog who was supposed to be well-trained and I got this! How can you sell people service dogs that act this way?'

"And Lisa just stares at us for a second. The look on her face—totally shocked. 'You think—? You think he's one of *ours*?'

"The way she said that. . ." Jordan shakes his head. "I think that's when I knew."

"Oh, no," Tanya breathes.

Jordan nods. "'I'm sorry,' Lisa says, 'but we've never seen this dog before.'"

He swallows, swipes at the sweat on his forehead. "Could I maybe have a glass of water?" His scent has changed. Not a lot, but it's different somehow. Not sure why.

Molly gives him a sharp look. "Sure. Are you okay? Do you need to check your blood sugar or anything?"

"I'm okay," he snaps. But then, after a pause, the air goes out of him. "Maybe I better. I promised Mama I'd check more often." He pulls a cloth container from his pocket.

Molly hands my leash to Tanya and says, "Be right back."

Jordan unzips the container and takes out a small pill container and what looks like a tiny machine. From the pill container, he pulls out a skinny stiff strip of paper and sticks it into the tiny machine. It beeps. Then he pricks one of his fingers causing it to bleed and lifts the little machine so that the end of the paper strip touches the blood. The machine beeps again.

Molly returns with bottles of water and hands one to Jordan and Tanya, keeping one for herself. A drink sounds good to me, too, but no chance of that probably.

But then Molly looks down at me and says, "Would you like a drink, Doodle? You're panting." Have I mentioned she's good at looking out for me? She starts for the door, but Jordan says, "Hey, I'm low. Guess it's good I checked. Could I get a Coke or something with sugar?"

"Yeah," Molly says, suddenly alarmed. She hustles through the door and returns with a can of soda under her chin and my water dish in her hands. She gives Jordan the can and sets my dish down in front of me.

Jordan pops open the can, tilts his head back and guzzles down a series of long swallows. I lap my water. And then he burps. "Sorry." He gives the girls an apologetic look.

Molly watches him anxiously. "Do you need some food? Or another drink?"

"Should we call your mama?" Tanya asks, worried as well.

Jordan shakes his head. "I'm fine. This will bring it back up. It's just that sometimes I can't feel when it drops, and that's when it's dangerous."

"Like the other day," Molly says.

He nods.

Tanya, still looking worried, says, "Good thing you checked!"

"Yeah," Jordan admits. "That's why I need a service dog. I can't always tell when my blood sugar gets too low, but a dog can smell it, and then they train the dog to alert."

Come to think of it, Jordan's scent is a little different now. Like it was when he first came.

"I have to take insulin," Jordan says, "and sometimes it's hard to get the amount exactly right. And too much makes my blood sugar too low." He tilts the can again and finishes off its contents.

Tanya leans forward in her chair. "What happened? After Lisa said Cooper wasn't their dog?"

"Well, this man comes in from the backroom. Older with graying hair. Dressed in jeans and T-shirt. Looks, I don't know, important. 'I heard barking,' he says. 'What's going on?'

"Of course, Cooper goes ballistic again, but the man takes the leash and calms him down. Lisa suddenly seems nervous and flustered. 'A mistake,' she says.

"'We made a mistake?' the man asks. He gets Cooper to lie down. Cooper really seems to like him

"Lisa shakes her head. 'No. They did. Come to the wrong place.' All her friendliness is gone. She glares at Mama as if it's all her fault.

"Mama takes the contract and shoves it at Lisa. 'You can't get away with that. We have a contract.'

"'Contract?' The man grabs the papers out of Lisa's hand. 'This is our letterhead,' he says, frowning. He reads through the pages and shakes his head as if he can't believe it. He turns to Cooper. 'I've never seen this dog before.'

"'I know,' Lisa says. 'They've made a mistake. I can handle it.'

"The man looks at her like she's crazy. He pulls out his phone and texts someone, and then makes a call, walking out of the room for a second. When he comes back in, he tells Lisa he's going to call the police and LSSC's attorney."

Jordan takes a few swallows of water.

"Wow!" Tanya says and Molly nods agreement.

Setting down the bottle, Jordan continues. "Finally, the man, his face all grim, says to Mama, 'I think we might have been spoofed. I think someone sold you a dog pretending it was from us.'"

"Spoofed?" Tanya asks.

"That's what we said. What's that? And the man says, 'It's when someone—usually a hacker online—sends emails that pretend to be from well-known companies to try to get information from people.'

"He looks at the contract again. 'You paid $15,000?'

"'Yeah,' Mama tells him, 'and most of it came from our church. They had a bunch of fund raisers.' This seems to make Lisa and the man even more upset.

"Lisa says, 'Oh, no! I'm so sorry.' But she looks more nervous than sad. 'We don't sell our dogs. We get grants to fund the cost for the people we provide with dogs.'

"'Well, it said on your website the fee is $15,000. And that's where I got his name, how I contacted Kirby Banes.' Mama says. 'Something fishy is going on here.'

"'On the website?' Now the man looks even more worried. Scared almost. 'So they spoofed us there, too?'

"'Don't ask me,' Mama says. 'All I know is I'm out a lot of money from your place, money a lot of good people worked hard to get, and all I've got is a dog that's not doing his job for a kid with a serious health problem.'

"And right as she says that, Cooper starts barking again, like he's proving her point. It was almost funny," Jordan says, a bit of a smile starting on his face. Then it fades. "Except it wasn't."

"That makes more sense," Tanya says. "That they spoofed the website as well. So it all looked okay. But how did they get all the forms and stuff the guy had when he came to your house?"

Molly gives Tanya an appreciative look. "I was wondering that, too." She frowns. "Is Cooper microchipped? Service dogs usually are."

"Yeah. Mr. Banes said he was microchipped and had all his shots, that he was ready for his new home."

"Did you call the microchip company and register the chip in your name?" Molly asks.

Jordan stares at her. "Mr. Banes didn't say anything about that."

"He should have!" Molly says. "Otherwise, if Cooper gets lost and a shelter scans his chip, how will they know how to contact you?"

Jordan frowns. "I never thought about that."

"On the other hand . . ." Tanya shoots Molly a triumphant glance. "This might be the clue we need to find Kirby!"

"How?" Jordan asks, his frown deepening.

"The chip should be registered with the company who made it," Molly says. "So we can maybe see who bought the chip and see who is registered as the owner."

Jordan thinks about it for a second, then grimaces. "If he wasn't lying about there being one."

"Well, yeah," Molly says glumly. Then, brightening, "But Annie has a microchip reader so we can check."

When Jordan looks uncertain, Tanya touches his arm. "It's a start. Mama always says it's better to have more information than less."

Molly nods. "And Annie will be here tonight. You could bring Cooper over. Or maybe she could come by your place."

"Okay." Jordan smiles for the first time since he's been here. "This is great. You guys are great."

He finishes his water. Then, looking embarrassed, he asks, "Could I use your bathroom?" He fingers the empty Coke can and water bottle.

"Sure." Molly jumps up, once again handing my leash to Tanya. "I'll show you where it is."

While they're gone, Tanya strokes me under my chin. Have I mentioned the Franklins are some of my favorite people?

When they come back, Jordan is saying, "I have some money saved up from last summer—I mowed my neighbor's lawn, so I could pay her."

Tanya gives Molly a puzzled look.

"He's wondering about hiring Annie to train Cooper to be more obedient," Molly tells her. Turning to Jordan, she says, "I already asked if she could help. Right now, she's completely swamped with the wedding. But afterward she probably could."

Jordan sighs, clearly disappointed. "That's okay. I just thought if Mama could see that Cooper was improving . . ." He twirls the water bottle in his hand. "She's talking about getting rid of him."

"I'll see if she could squeeze in one lesson before the wedding," Molly says. "She's really busy, so I don't know."

Jordan's eyes light up. "That'd be great." He stands up. "I'd better get home before Mama thinks I've passed out again."

He thanks Molly and Tanya and they all exchange phone numbers. And then he leaves, his footsteps thudding gently on the sidewalk.

Chapter 7

Getting to Know the Neighbors

When Annie arrives to eat the leftover enchiladas with us, Molly tells her about Jordan's visit. She already gave the boss the whole story right after Jordan left, but she goes through it all again. Annie listens without interrupting except when Molly gets to the part about Jordan needing a Coke for his blood sugar. Not exactly sure what blood sugar is, except it seems important to humans.

"So he can't tell when it's getting too low?" Annie asks, a forkful of enchilada paused mid-air.

"Sometimes he can't. That's what happened yesterday when he was chasing after Cooper. He didn't know until he started to pass out, and then it was too late." Molly takes a sip of her soda.

"There's a term for that." Annie frowns, thinking. "Hypoglycemic unawareness. If he has that, he definitely could use a diabetic alert dog. Could save his life."

"I don't think Cooper will be it," the boss says.

"Maybe he could be if he gets trained right," Molly says. "Jordan wants to give him a chance."

"A chance to let him go into a coma?" the boss asks skeptically.

Molly gives him a look and continues the story. When she gets to the part about the microchip, the boss says, "You're signing Annie up for lots of things to do."

Molly bites her lip. "Just the scan—which could help us find the guy who scammed them—and maybe one lesson before you go?" She gives Annie an anxious look. "Is that too much? Jordan texted me and said it would be okay with his mom."

Annie sighs. "I guess. If I can find the scanner without opening a thousand boxes. I brought it over a few days ago. But—" she meets Molly's eyes "—nothing more until after the wedding! It'll take me a month to recover. Maybe two."

Molly nods. "Cross my heart," she says earnestly.

Annie's face softens the same way the boss's does sometimes. "You have a good heart, Molly. You don't need to cross it."

Molly flushes and for a moment no one speaks. Then the boss rises, carrying his plate to the sink. "Maybe you can do the dishes while Annie looks for the scanner."

"Okay," Molly says without enthusiasm. "We should have trained Doodle to find more things so he could help us unpack."

The boss gives me a speculative look. "We should have trained him to do dishes!"

They all laugh although I'm not sure what is funny.

Molly starts on the dishes, while I nap on the kitchen floor. Before long, Annie announces that she's found the scanner. Molly sends a text to Jordan.

"I'll do a little work with Cooper," Annie says on her way out the door. "See what's going on with him. So I'll be maybe a half hour or forty-five minutes."

"We'll be here," the boss says, "our heads bowed over boxes, slowly asphyxiating from the dust."

Annie laughs and soon I hear her truck leave the driveway.

My bed is still upright against the wall, so I nap on the rug in Molly's room while she puts away clothes.

I'm startled awake when the doorbell rings. I give a surprised woof. I didn't hear a car or even footsteps.

"Who can that be?" the boss asks, echoing my thoughts.

He goes to the door and opens it.

A stout woman with very short hair and bug-like eyes behind rimless glasses stands on our porch. She smells of sweat and Cheetos, an odd substance people seem to think is food. She's wearing shorts so tight her thighs bulge out at the seams. "What's going on here?" she asks, glowering at the boss.

"Excuse me?" the boss asks. Molly comes up behind him and stares at the woman open-mouthed. I move a little in front of her, of course, in case the woman might be an intruder.

"What are you doing in this house?" the woman demands.

"Excuse me?" the boss says again, as if he can't believe what he's hearing. "Who are you?"

"Chris Dodds," the woman snaps. "I live down the street. Who are you?"

Her voice is so belligerent that my hair rises on my back. I can smell the boss's tension, but he keeps his voice calm. "Josh Turner. We just moved in."

"What?" She sounds surprised and angry. "How'd that happen?"

The boss rubs his beard and takes a breath. "In the usual way. I put down a deposit and signed a lease." His voice has developed a decided edge. "What do you want?"

"Margaret leased it to *you*? Why would she do that?"

I can smell the boss's anger. "I don't think that's any of your business," the boss says his voice now frigid. "What do you want?"

"What I want is this place. Margaret as good as promised that I could rent it when Mrs. Johnson died. I've wanted to move here for years." Her big eyes, intent on the boss, remind me of a chihuahua about to snap at someone's hand.

The boss returns her stare. "I'm afraid I can't help you. We signed a year's lease with an option to renew in a year." He starts to close the door, but the woman thrusts an arm forward.

"You don't understand. I was *promised* this place. We're cooped up in that tiny one-bedroom apartment and ever since Ryan moved in, it's been practically unlivable. Margaret told me I could have this after Mrs. Johnson passed. Ryan's having to sleep on the couch."

For a moment, the boss and the woman just stare at each other. I watch her carefully, the hair still raised on my back. She's acting very much like an intruder and I don't want to be taken by surprise.

Then, the woman's eyes narrow. "So what'd you do? Offer her twice as much as it's worth or something? One of these rich yuppies who think they'll gentrify the neighborhood? How much a month are you paying?"

"None of your business." The boss's voice is gruff, angry. He pushes the door against her hand. "You need to leave. Now."

For a moment, the woman resists, but then pulls her arm away. "You haven't heard the end of this," she says. "Not by a long shot."

The door closes with a thud, and the boss flips the latch on the lock.

"Wow," Molly says. "What's with her?"

The boss slowly shakes his head. "Welcome to the neighborhood. What a piece of work."

They go back to unpacking. Sometime later, I hear Annie's truck. And after a few moments, a knock on the door.

"I forgot it's locked!" the boss says, bounding across the room to turn the latch.

"You locked it?" Annie asks, surprised.

"Yeah. We had a friendly neighborly visit."

Molly says "If that was friendly . . ."

Annie gives them both a questioning look.

The boss tells her about the strange neighbor, including her threats at the end.

Annie shakes her head. "I hate having to deal with adults who've never grown up," she says.

What? The woman looked grown up to me.

"What's with everyone wanting our house?" Molly asks indignantly. "First Mrs. Thomas's son and now this lady."

"With what sounds like her deadbeat son," the boss says. "It's no mystery. Arlington is one of the highest priced places to live in the nation. So any rental that seems even remotely affordable, well, everyone wants it. We'd probably live somewhere else if it weren't for your school."

At this, Molly stiffens a little.

Annie, her face drooping with exhaustion, flops down on a portion of the couch that doesn't have a box. "It might take me more than a couple of months to recover. Maybe a year."

The boss shifts a couple of boxes and sits beside her, beckoning Molly to his free side. When she scoots up next to him, he puts his arms around her and Annie.

Molly turns to Annie. "So, did Cooper have a chip?"

Annie nods. "He did, so at least that part of the Kirby Banes story was true. Keira and Jordan are going to try to trace it, although I'm not sure they know what they're doing."

"I can help," Molly says eagerly.

"Yeah, that'd be good. I . . ." Annie closes her eyes. "I certainly don't have the time or the energy."

"How'd Cooper do with the training?" the boss asks. "Does he have service dog potential?"

Annie sighs. "Maybe in a few years. But he's just too young. He's at the age where he should be just starting a six-month training program, not placed in a home where a kid could pass out if he doesn't do his job." Another sigh. "Too young and way too energetic. I think he might make a decent search dog—search and rescue, or maybe even mold or bed bugs. Something that requires energy. Right now, he's a handful."

Molly pushes herself up from the couch. "Can I have the number? I'll go check on it."

"Sure." Annie pulls out her phone. Molly runs into her room and comes back with a piece of paper and a pen. She writes as Annie dictates a long number and then returns to her computer.

The boss and Annie snuggle on the couch. Her head is on his shoulder and her eyes are closed. His eyes have that dreamy, happy look he has had a lot lately.

I curl down on my rug in Molly's room for a nap. But I'm barely starting to dream when Molly shouts, "Got it! I found the company who has Cooper's microchip!"

The boss and Annie get up and come into her bedroom. Molly points at the monitor. "Always Together. And it says they have twenty-four-hour service. I'm going to call them." She carefully taps her phone a bunch of times and then says, "I'm putting it on speaker." She taps one more time and once again the grating sound phones make when calling gets loud. It goes on for some time and Molly's face falls. She sighs. But then the grating stops.

"Always Together," a crisp female voice says.

Molly swallows. "I'm calling about a dog we found that's registered with Always Together."

The boss raises his eyebrows at this, but Molly's attention is on her monitor. "I can give you the number," she says. When the woman tells her to go ahead, Molly dictates a long string of numbers. Somehow, these numbers help people find lost dogs. I've never understood how, but this whole microchip thing can prove who owns a dog, something we recently discovered can be really important. But, as so often with these things, it's all beyond my comprehension.

After a pause, the woman says, "Yes, he is registered with us."

Molly gives a thumbs up to the boss, grinning now.

"We will let the registered owner know you've found the dog. Could I have your contact information so the owner can call you?"

Molly's excitement fades. "You can't give me the phone number? It'd be much quicker."

"I'm sorry. We can't give that information out. But we will inform the owner immediately and he or she should get back to you right away."

Molly gives the woman her name and phone number and the boss's name and phone as well. She flips her phone shut.

The boss shakes his head. "Boy, they're being cagey. 'He or she' will get back to you? They can't even say if it's a man or woman?"

"Well, they are protecting the owner's privacy," Annie says, "something we could use more of. Let's just hope the owner gets back to us. If 'he or she' doesn't, we won't be any further along than we were before." She yawns. "I've got to get home. What time are we meeting Reverend Henry?"

"Nine," the boss answers.

Annie grimaces. "It'll feel like the crack of dawn." She gives the boss a quick kiss and then she's out the door.

Molly goes back to her computer, almost always boring, so I curl down to resume my nap.

I wake up to the sound of the boss's phone buzzing.

"Oh, Mrs. Thomas. Hi. What's up?"

Molly sits up straight, stiffening. She goes into the living room and stands next to the boss. I follow, of course.

I don't know what's up, but the boss looks worried, the scent of his tension suddenly in the air.

"I hope I haven't called too late." Mrs. Thomas's voice comes over the phone. Molly leans in, listening.

"No. Not at all." His voice is stringy with tension. "Just unpacking."

She laughs. "That's an endless job isn't it? I'm calling to see if you'd like another job. I have some rentals in Falls Church, and one of the tenants there thinks he might have bed bugs. I wondered what you'd charge to take that fine dog of yours over there and check it out."

The boss blinks and his mouth moves for a moment without any sound. Then he clears his throat. "Sure, we'd be glad to check it out. We can go by tomorrow if you like. Let me know what time will be acceptable to the tenant and we'll be there."

"That'd be wonderful," Mrs. Thomas says. "What are your rates?"

"Well," the boss still looking uncertain, hesitates. "We'd be glad to do it for free."

This surprises me. The boss doesn't generally like to do things for free.

"We're very . . . grateful to have this house. We love it here. It's the least we can do."

There's a brief silence on the other end of the line, and then in a dry voice, "You're going to continue paying rent, aren't you? And do the repairs we talked about?"

"Of course!" the boss splutters, now looking surprised.

"Well, that's all you owe me. Not free work."

"It's just that . . ." The boss sighs. "We got a visit from a neighbor earlier. She seems to think you promised this place to her."

"Oh, dear." Mrs. Thomas chuckles. "Would that be Chris Dodds perhaps?"

"Yeah," the boss says, his eyes dark with worry.

"She's been after this place since I moved out umpteen years ago," Mrs. Thomas says. "Thinks I ought to give to her because we once were neighbors. But last I looked, I'm the one who pays taxes on this place and I get to decide who's in it. Not Chris Dodds and not my son, God bless him. You keep your end of our agreement and we're fine."

The boss lets out a long breath. "Well, thanks. As I said, we love the place!" After a short pause, the boss gives her our rates, although they somehow seem different. He arranges to meet her at the rental, says goodbye. and clicks off, looking a little stunned.

"I thought she was calling to tell us it was all off. I thought maybe that Dodds lady convinced her she should have the place." He shakes his head, his face still pale.

"I know. That's what I thought, too," Molly says. "But you have a contract."

"Yeah, but she could make life miserable for us if she wanted us out. And even if she honored it, if she wanted us out, we'd have to move in a year." He gestures to the boxes. "I don't want to do this again in a year. Or ever." He shuts his eyes, takes a deep breath, and then smiles. "Glad I was wrong. I really like Mrs. Thomas. Class act."

He glances down at me. "Doodle, it looks like we have a job."

Molly says, "Yeah, for half your normal rate!"

The boss, looking sheepish—a weird term that I learned has more to do with embarrassment than sheep, which can only be a good thing—smiles again. "Well, let's just say Mrs. Thomas isn't the only one who can give someone a good deal."

Chapter 8

Practice, Practice, Practice

I DON'T NORMALLY GO TO CHURCH, WHICH IS FINE BY ME because, frankly, it's not all that interesting to dogs. Talk, talk, talk, if you get my drift. Okay, sometimes there can be singing but when the music starts, dogs aren't welcome to join in. Learned *that* the hard way.

True, in some churches they pass around plates of bread—saw that in my service dog days—but, as usual, we were strictly forbidden to take any. In other churches, the people go up a take a little cracker from a man in a robe at the front. Again—dogs not welcome.

Not sure if this will be a bread or cracker place, but we're in the parking lot of a brick, pointy roofed, colored windowed church that looks much like a smaller version of other churches in the area. We're here for what the boss calls a quick walk-through so that he and Annie know what's going on before we have the official rehearsal, when everyone is in town. Turns out that people have to practice getting married. At the least, the boss and Annie think they do, and they think Molly and Tanya and us dogs need to practice our part, too.

Only gone to one wedding myself, back when I was training to be a service dog. It was held in a vast church with high ceilings and echoing sound and filled with lots of dressed-up people wearing enough perfume and cologne to render a poor dog's nose useless. Lots of music, too, with a few people getting up and singing at some points in the service. And then a lot of people marching down the length of the church—more perfume and cologne, alas—and a minister who talked for some time. Not exactly the most exciting thing a dog could do with his time, if you ask me, which no one did.

All in all, it was quite complicated, which I guess is why there needs to be a practice. Kind of like a dog show, where everyone has to learn where to stand and where to walk.

The boss, who has been checking his phone every few minutes, sighs with relief. "Annie and Tanya are almost here. The traffic's cleared out now."

The boss isn't the only one constantly checking his phone. Molly keeps pulling hers out of her pocket and sneaking anxious glances at the screen. She's even more worried than the boss, the scents of tension pouring from her. Unlike the boss, she doesn't relax at the news about Annie.

Before long, Annie zips into the parking lot. She's driving her little car, a tiny one she got not long ago because it gets better mileage, a term I don't quite understand. Usually dressed in jeans and a long-sleeved shirt, this morning Annie's wearing slacks and a shiny sleeveless top and what Molly calls flats rather than her usual sneakers. Tanya is with her, and so is Chloe. Annie leads Chloe from the back seat and hands the leash to Tanya.

We're good friends, Chloe and me, and after we sniff our greetings, Chloe bows to invite me to play.

"Not now," Tanya says firmly, tightening Chloe's leash. Annie nods her approval. She's been working with Tanya on dog handling.

I push forward and bow back at Chloe. Molly, who has my leash, says, "No! Sit!" I sit.

The boss shakes his head. "I'm still not wild about the idea of having the dogs here."

"They'll be fine," Annie, Molly, and Tanya all say at the same time, which makes them laugh.

The boss consults his phone. "Reverend Henry said he'd be here at nine so we're a little early."

The boss tells us this rehearsal is being squeezed in around Reverend Henry's other appointments. "He's a busy guy."

Molly and Tanya take Chloe and me to the lawn and invite us to pee, which, after some searching for the right spot, we do.

"Your mom hasn't answered yet?" Tanya asks, when Molly checks her phone again.

Molly glances at the boss, and says in a low voice, "Not yet. And Dad says they need to know for sure how many are coming. But I don't want to nag her, you know?"

Tanya nods sympathetically. "I can see how your mom might want to come to see you, but maybe doesn't because she'll be sad that she's alone."

"I know," Molly says miserably. "I'm not sure it was a great idea to invite her at all. But I didn't want her to feel left out. And lots of exes come to weddings these days."

We walk back to the parking lot where the boss and Annie are.

An aged sedan sporting a couple of dents and a little rust on the bumper pulls into the parking lot.

"Right on time," the boss says, going over to the car.

The man who gets out is older than the boss, maybe Mr. Franklin's age. Like Mr. Franklin, his hair is curly and starting to show white, but he has less of it and is mostly bald on top. He's wearing dark shiny shoes, suit pants, and a short-sleeved shirt with one those stiff collars common to ministers. He smells of pipe tobacco, a scent I don't come across too often, coffee, and, oddly, a little of popcorn.

The boss goes over to offer his hand. "Josh Hunter," he says. "Nice to meet you in person, Reverend Henry."

"I believe I've seen you in church before," Reverend Henry says, smiling as he shakes the boss's hand. He has a low, almost gravelly voice.

"We've come a few times with the Franklins," the boss replies.

"To hear Tanya sing," Molly adds, bending her head toward Tanya.

"The voice of an angel," Reverend Henry states fervently. Tanya looks embarrassed.

The boss introduces Molly and Annie.

"And this is Doodle and Chloe," Molly adds.

Reverend Henry gazes down at us. "Handsome dogs."

"And well-trained," Molly says, with a sidelong glance at the boss.

"Well, let's show you the church." Reverend Henry leads us across the lawn and to the main doors, which he unlocks. He flips on a light switch and takes us through a small room to a bigger one that has rows of shiny wooden benches on either side of a center carpeted aisle. The windows are the colored kind that show pictures.

"Oh, this is lovely!" Annie breathes, eyes wide. "I love the stained glass."

"I thought you'd like it," the boss says, happy.

Before long, the boss, Annie, and Reverend Henry are deep in conversation about guests, and how the service will work. Chloe and I lie at Molly and Tanya's feet, both of us working our noses. Molly checks her phone a time or two.

"How many guests do you suppose you'll have?" Reverend Henry gestures at the church. "Just making sure they'll fit in this space."

"We're keeping it small," Annie answers. "My mother and sister, Josh's parents and his brother's family, the Franklins . . ." she sucks in a lip, frowning as she glances at Molly.

"Along with a few friends," the boss adds. "And maybe Molly's mother and some of her family." He turns to Molly. "Have you heard anything?"

Molly's face colors and she shakes her head.

The boss's lips tighten. "I hope she lets us know before the actual day. I mean—"

"I *know*," Molly snaps. She pulls out her phone, stares at it a second, then shoves it back into her pocket. "I texted her this morning, but she hasn't answered."

Annie, glancing at Molly, says, "We haven't heard from them yet, but the total count won't be over forty."

Reverend Henry's deep voice exudes calm. "I don't think that will matter. We've got plenty of room for the number you're expecting. You could add another ten or fifteen people and it'd be just fine." He gives Molly a friendly look.

I like this man. He smiles a lot, but unlike many people who do so, his smiles seem genuine. And he has a calm presence that makes me want to be near him. "That will be just perfect," he says.

He leads us to the front of the church and gestures to the boss and Annie. "You two will stand here, in front of the altar." They take their positions.

"And Miss Tanya and Miss Molly," he says.

Molly pockets her phone, snapping to attention.

"You and the dogs will already be up front, and will be waiting here, to the side of Mr. Hunter."

Molly leads me to the position he indicates, and Tanya does the same with Chloe.

"Perfect," he says, with another big smile. "These are very good dogs."

Molly shoots the boss another look.

"And that's it," Reverend Henry says. He turns and starts toward the main entry. "Let me show you the staging area." We all follow him to the little entry way we came through earlier. "As you can see, the space here is limited and you'll have to gather outside first. Let's hope it's not raining."

"Not supposed to," Annie says and for some reason knocks on the wood door.

Reverend Henry smiles again. "Good. So, it's all pretty simple. We'll go into more detail at the rehearsal." He leads us back through the main doors, locking them behind him.

Everyone says goodbye, and then we split up. Molly gets in Annie's car with Tanya and Chloe. The boss puts on my working vest—the one that has a picture of a bed bug with a line through it—before loading me in my crate, and we head out to do a job.

He plugs his phone into the dashboard, and soon I hear that smooth female voice talking to him. It's a one-way conversation, "turn right at the next intersection," that sort of thing, and I gather he's getting directions. From where, of course, I haven't a clue.

The voice takes us to a neighborhood mostly made up of brick apartment complexes. We slow down next to a smaller one sitting between two much larger buildings. Hey, Mrs. Thomas is here, her little car parked on the street. She gives us a nod, and we pull up and park behind her.

"Good morning," she says, walking up to us as the boss is getting me out of my crate.

"Good morning," the boss replies. He grabs his workbag and locks the door. "Going to be a hot one, I think."

Mrs. Thomas agrees. Worrying about the weather is definitely a human rather than a dog thing, and something they do often.

Most of the buildings on the street are dark brick, but this one is gray with pillars supporting a covered porch, painted the same color, and bordered with a light wood rail frame. The entrance to the porch is on the side, next to a narrow driveway that has several parked cars at the far end. There are two doors, one at either end of the porch, and a round table with several chairs between them.

"Bought this, oh, thirty-five years ago," Mrs. Thomas is saying. She walks stiff-kneed up the wooden porch steps, the way older people do. "Raymond got a great deal on it, and it's been a good investment for us, but even so, we had to borrow the down payment, and oh did we scrimp those first few years to make the payments." She shakes her head. "Mercy. Those were hard times, but good, you know?" She gives the building a fond glance. "And it paid off."

"Denzel wants me to sell it," she continues. "Because of my health, he says. My health is just fine, thank you very much, at least for my age. He says I should get my money out now because real estate has appreciated so much."

"Gone through the roof, all right," the boss agrees whole-heartedly.

I glance up at the roof, but don't see anything.

"He keeps telling me to sell it and use the money while I'm still alive. Take a cruise. Go to Europe." She gives the boss a crooked smile. "But I don't need more money. And I don't want to take a cruise or go to Europe. And I can't help thinking what he's really hoping is that I'll give him some of it."

She sighs. "Anyway, it's reaching the point where maintenance costs are high, but even so, the rent is higher." Her face twitches into another brief smile. "It's still a good investment, especially now that it's paid off, but Denzell seems to have missed the business sense that Raymond and I had when we were young. He's certainly missed the idea of scrimping to be able to buy something. Raymond and I wanted him to have more than we had as children, and he did, but now I wonder if that was actually a good thing."

"I know what you mean," the boss says. "I try not to give Molly too much, but it's hard."

Mrs. Thomas nods sympathetically, then knocks on one of the doors.

It's opened almost immediately by a pear-shaped Latino man with wispy gray hair on top of a bald scalp. He's wearing loose pants and slippers and smells of garlic.

"Good morning, Mr. Lopez." Mrs. Thomas smiles at him and introduces the boss, and then we go inside.

I don't immediately catch the scent of bed bugs, which I sometimes do if there's a heavy infestation, but that doesn't mean they aren't here.

"Thanks for coming," Mr. Lopez says. "I've got these bites on my legs." He bends down and starts to pull up one leg of his pants, but then changes his mind. "I guess you don't need to see." He turns to me and his face breaks into a big smile. "Oh, is this the famous bed bug dog?" He reaches out as if to pet me, but then pulls back his arm. "Is it okay?" he asks.

"Sure," the boss says. "He likes to be stroked under the chin."

I stand still while the man stoops to pet me. "What a great dog!"

The boss likes to say that I'm a good-will ambassador for his business. I'm not sure what he means, but his clients like it when they can pet me. Service dogs aren't supposed to be petted because it distracts them from their job. Fortunately, the boss says, when it comes to petting, bed bug dogs are a different breed. Which is odd, because there are plenty of labradoodles who are service dogs and plenty who are bed bug dogs.

After Mr. Lopez straightens back up, the boss says, "Okay, we're going to get to work here." He gives me my command and I put my nose to the floor, an old wooden one, scratched and somewhat dusty, and begin the search. Nothing in the living room.

We go straight back into a small kitchen with white cupboards and appliances and a somewhat curling linoleum floor. The kitchen has a back door leading to a tiny laundry room, which has a door that leads outside to a straggly line of grass, bounded by a sagging wooden fence. Nothing in the kitchen either, but I catch a whiff of the bed bug scent in the laundry room, under a new-looking washing machine.

"The washer's working great," Mr. Lopez says to Mrs. Thomas. "So much better than the old one! Thank you so much."

"Oh good," Mrs. Thomas says, sounding happy. To the boss,

she says, "We had to replace it a few weeks ago. Denzel delivered it for me."

I'm still sniffing the suspicious spot. The boss watches with interest but doesn't move or say anything. He's careful about not interfering with my searches. To pass the NABBS exam—that's a test the boss and I have to take to make sure we can really find bed bugs—a handler cannot give the dog any kind of help. It's kind of a silly rule because if the boss knew where the bugs were he wouldn't need me, right? So how much help can he be? Still, he's always careful, in his words, to "not contaminate the search."

The problem here is that there is a definite scent of bed bugs under the washer, but not of live ones. I've been trained only to find live ones, another skill I have to show during the NABBS exams. I sniff until I'm certain the scent is only of dead ones, and we move on to a small bedroom.

I go straight to the bed, the favorite choice of bed bugs. Bingo! There are some here. Not very many by the smell of it, but definitely some live ones. I alert, the boss pays me with liver treats—so tasty—and he begins his visual search. He lifts up the mattress and inspects the seams carefully. At one point, I shove my nose into a spot to help him out.

"Ah, yes," he says. "Good dog."

I get another treat.

"There are a few here," the boss says to Mr. Lopez, who absentmindedly starts scratching his leg. The boss shows him the evidence of bed bug poop hidden in the mattress seams. "But not very many. I don't think they've been here for long."

After we've thoroughly inspected the bed, he has me search the molding around the floor. Often, especially in a heavy infestation, colonies of the bugs will live in the walls. But I find no trace of the bugs anywhere else in the room, or indeed in the other bedroom or bathroom.

When we're finished, we all go back into the living room. Mrs. Thomas sits on the couch and Mr. Lopez on a stuffed chair. The boss remains standing.

"Well, you definitely have a few. But as I said, it looks like a light infestation. It shouldn't be too hard to get rid of them if they're only in this apartment. But if they're in the other three, then it will be harder. We need to check them to find out."

Mrs. Thomas looks up at him in surprise. "None of the other tenants have said anything," she says, not looking happy.

"They might not know. Sometimes, especially this time of year, they might think the bites are from chiggers or even fleas. But if we don't check the other apartments, you could pay to have someone exterminate them here, only to have the bugs come back."

"Do you have time to check the others while you're here?" Mrs. Thomas asks. "I could see if the tenants are willing. I know Mr. Sato next door won't mind. He and his cat are both older than Methuselah and happy to have any kind of company. But I'll need to contact the upstairs tenants."

"Of course," the boss says. "I have a list of pest control companies in the van, if you'd like."

"I've used Arnie's for years. Always do a good job."

Mrs. Thomas gets on the phone and spends several minutes talking. Then she says, "We can go ahead with all of them but need to do Nicole last. She's in the one right above here. She has a toddler, so she'd like a few minutes to straighten up."

Mrs. Thomas says goodbye to Mr. Lopez, who stands in his doorway and watches her knock on another door. An elderly Japanese man leaning on a cane opens it.

"Good morning, Mr. Sato," Mrs. Thomas says.

She introduces the boss, and she and Mr. Sato talk for a minute or two. Then she says to the boss, "If you don't mind, I'm going to go sit down here and see about getting Arnie's to send someone out."

Mr. Sato's face crinkles into a broad smile and he welcomes us inside with a small bow. In the way of some apartments, this one looks like the other one but backwards. A cat, every bit as thin and old as the man, hides under the couch. In fact, the whole apartment smells of cat.

His place is full of house plants, some hanging and several large ones in big pots by the windows.

"I never thought dogs could find bed bugs," he says, beaming down at me. "Amazing what dogs can do these days, isn't it?"

The boss smiles and agrees.

Seriously? It's not that we can suddenly do these things, but that humans have discovered how to use our superior noses to help them find things. But, as I mentioned, the boss tries to be super friendly to the residents of the places we search. "We're looking for something they hope we won't find," he always says, "so the more we can sugarcoat the medicine, the easier it goes down."

That last part always loses me, but the gist is that even if the people we meet make stupid statements about dogs, he doesn't disagree with them.

The cat growls at me when I search the couch but doesn't move. I don't find any bed bugs or even any fleas, not always a given when there are cats around. Dogs can get fleas, too, I'm sad to admit, but the boss has me wear a collar that keeps them away.

When we're done there, Mrs. Thomas takes us around to the back building and points to a staircase that leads to a narrow porch that runs the length of the building. "Do the one on the right first," she says. "I'm going to save my knees and stay down here."

We search the two upstairs apartments but find no bed bugs. The one with the young mother has plenty of the urine and poop smells that go hand-in-hand with toddlers, but no insects of any kind.

Mrs. Thomas seems delighted by the news. "Good," she says. "I have Arnie's coming this afternoon. They said if the infestation is as light as you say, I probably won't need to replace the mattress."

She hands the boss a check which he pockets without looking at it, and we all walk to our cars.

When we get back home, we find Annie putting away things in the kitchen and Molly sitting in front of her computer monitor.

The boss drops his bag on the floor of the bedroom that is going to be his office, and then takes off my vest. I shake to straighten out my fur.

"How'd it go?" Annie asks when we join her in the kitchen.

"Good." The boss pulls out the check Mrs. Thomas gave him, glances at it, and then holds it up his face. "That woman," he says, shaking his head.

"What?" Annie asks with alarm.

"She made it for twice what I quoted her."

"So, your normal rate then?" Annie asks.

"Yeah. I don't know how she knew, but I guess she did." He shakes his head again. "As I said, she's a class act."

Molly bursts into the kitchen. "Guess what?"

Annie looks like she knows the answer.

"She called! Cooper's original owner called!"

The boss's eyebrows raise.

"I was afraid she wouldn't, you know? But right after we got home from the church thing, my phone rang and it was this woman, Celia Stewart. She's a college student who got him as a puppy, but then when he was six months old, decided he was too hard to keep." She glances at Annie. "Like you said always happens."

Annie sighs. "I told Molly earlier that's the story of half the dogs in shelters. Cute pup becomes difficult adolescent."

"So Cooper wasn't registered by the kennel," the boss says. "Why am I not surprised?"

Molly nods quickly. "Anyway, Celia said she put an ad on Craigslist and this man came and bought him. But guess what?"

"What?" the boss says with a glance at Annie and a slight smile.

"I asked her the man's name. She had to look it up, but then she found it." She gives the boss a triumphant look. "Kirby Banes."

"Really!" The boss looks impressed. "The one and the same. Good work!"

"Celia said he was really nice and was scouting for dogs for a service-dog company, and he thought Cooper—only Celia called him Jack—might work. But he didn't want to pay the price she was asking. Celia said he gave her this long story about how the service-dog organization depends on donations and how they need to find their dogs as cheaply as possible, and how he wasn't sure if Jack would make it as a service dog, but for the right price he'd be willing to try him out."

"That sounds like a con," the boss says. "Did he say he was from Life Support Service Canines?"

Another quick nod. "Yeah. Celia didn't remember the name, but when I asked about Life Support, she said oh, yeah, that was it. Anyway, she said she ended up selling Jack, as she called him, to Kirby so he'd have a chance to be a service dog. Even though she only got about a fourth of her asking price. Kirby promised her either way, he'd make sure the dog got a good home."

"She just took his word for all of that?" Annie shakes her head.

"She said he had a card with his name that said Life Support Service Dogs."

"Anyone can print a card with anything on it," the boss says. "He could have been just going to re-sell him."

"Or he could have been a dog fighter," Annie says grimly.

Molly's eyes widen at this "Yeah. At least he wasn't that. But she said he paid in cash, which is also kind of weird. Anyway, he was supposed to change the contact information on the chip. Celia gave him a bill of sale and everything so he could do it. So she was upset about that."

"Did you tell her about Jordan?" the boss asked.

Molly shakes her head.

"She should know," the boss says. "So she won't be so naïve in the future."

"I think maybe Molly felt it wasn't her place to tell her," Annie says gently. "We don't actually have any proof."

Molly gives Annie a grateful glace. "Yeah. I didn't know what to say, you know? I didn't want to tell her the man was a crook, although I think she's might have suspected something. She told me she took a cell phone photo of him and 'Jack,' and he got all upset. Insisted she delete it. Something about maintaining privacy for clients. She said it didn't make sense, but he was so angry she pretended to do it. And she sent me the photo!"

The boss says, "Well, at least we know his history—Cooper's, I mean. And this Banes guy has been a fraud from the start." He gives Molly a hug. "You did a great job. If you don't become a detective when you grow up, I think you'll have missed your true calling."

"Maybe," Molly says, beaming at him. Her face grows serious. "But I might want to be a photographer."

"Or that," the boss agrees.

"Or both!" Annie gives Molly a thumbs up.

And Molly gets this big smile, looking like a pup who has just discovered food in his bowl. "Or both," she says.

Chapter 9

Intruder!

"Can I take your laptop?" Molly asks between bites of macaroni and cheese. A half-eaten hot dog sits on her plate and I have hopes it will end up in my stomach. "For when I'm at Mom's?"

The boss, surprised, shakes his head. "I don't think so. All my work records are on it. If something happened to it, it'd be a disaster."

"But you have backups, right?"

"Molly, I use it every day. If I had to reinstall all the programs and try to bring another computer up to speed—I'd lose a lot of work time."

"But what am I going to do all day long at Mom's?" She gives him a speculative look. "Maybe I could get my own laptop."

The boss frowns. "It's just for a week."

"A week's a long time. Mom will be at work during the day. And Benita takes naps because she's old."

Benita is Molly's aunt—a great-great aunt or something. Not great as in terrific, although Molly likes her a lot, but meaning something else from what I gather.

"And I'll have a ton of photos from the wedding. Well, not the wedding, but the reception. If I have a laptop, I could go through them. Plus, if I had my own laptop, I could take it to school sometimes. Lots of the kids in my class have laptops."

"We can't afford one right now."

"Can't you just charge it?" Molly asks. "You'll have lots of work after you get back."

The boss frowns. "You know I don't like to charge things I can't pay off."

"Just this once?" she asks, a bit of whine coming into her voice.

The boss regards her seriously. "A new one is just not in the budget right now. If maybe we could find a used one or someone might lend you one . . . Let me think about it. Do you want to search online for a used one?"

"Yeah," she says, suddenly energized.

"The cheaper the better," the boss says. "With all the expenses of the move and the wedding . . ." He sighs. "Which I know is pretty much all my stuff and not yours." He gives her an anxious look.

Molly doesn't seem to notice. "It'll have to have enough RAM for me to do photos," she says, "and be fast enough that I don't fall asleep between screens."

The boss, worry lining his face, says, "Well, see what you can find. Maybe I can squeeze in some of the jobs I had postponed before the wedding. I can always unpack afterward."

Molly grins at this and goes into her room.

"Endless expenses," the boss says under his breath. "If we can find one you can borrow, that'd be best," he calls out. "And maybe you can save up for one down the road."

"I'm saving for a new camera," Molly calls back. "I can't buy everything."

"Welcome to life," the boss says, in a low voice. "Welcome to reality."

He goes to his desk and makes a few calls and the next thing I know, he's talking to Annie.

"Hey," he says, getting up to shut the door. I squeeze into the room before it closes.

"Molly wants a laptop for when she's at her mother's." He recounts their conversation.

"Well, I can see why she'd want one," Annie says.

The boss grimaces. "It's such a bad time financially. I'm not sure what to do. Normally, I'd tell her to save up for it or at least contribute to it. But here we are spending all this money on ourselves—the wedding, the honeymoon . . . I guess I feel selfish for not saying sure, we can spend another seven or eight hundred for something you want."

"Surely you can find a cheaper one than that," Annie says, her voice soothing. "And all of this isn't just for us. Well, the honeymoon is, but the home and the expenses to get it fixed up—that's for her too."

"I guess," he says. "I'm not sure she sees it that way. I told her the best thing would be to borrow one. I could lend her mine, but I don't want to. Too much to lose if it got damaged."

"I'll ask around," Annie says quickly. "Maybe my sister. She's always upgrading her computers and might have an older laptop around."

The boss's eyes light up. "That's a good idea. I think my dad just got a new system. I'll ask him if he has an older one Molly could borrow. And I'm going to schedule some jobs I'd put off until after the wedding. Bring in a little extra cash."

"We can always finish unpacking after we get back," Annie says. "Should I come over so you don't have to take Molly?"

The boss doesn't like to leave Molly alone unless it's for a short time and he's not far away.

"That'd be wonderful!" he says.

"It's not like I don't have any boxes to unpack or anything."

They talk some more, but I drift off to sleep, waking when the boss reopens his door. I check on Molly, who's still on her computer. I curl down for another nap, this time in her room.

Later, at bedtime, when the boss takes me out to pee, the kitten tries to run into the house. The boss gently but firmly pushes her away with his foot. "Not happening," he says. I make a quick tour of the yard to make sure all is well before doing what the boss calls "my business." And then it's back inside to the rug in Molly's room for the night.

Until I wake up. Did I hear something? Definitely something, but faint. Hard to figure out. I listen, ears forward, not moving. And then I know. Footsteps. In front of the house. Very quiet footsteps, the sneaky kind an intruder might make. I hear several creaks and a muffled thud. What the heck? I jump up, barking and run to the front door.

A few moments later, the boss shouts, "Doodle, what the heck?"

My question exactly. What—or more likely who—is out there? I bark some more.

"Hush!" he commands, as he stumbles into the room looking half asleep. He turns on the porch light and looks out the window, staring for a moment. "Nothing out there, Bud. You're hallucinating."

What? There's definitely something out there. I bark to let him know.

He flips the light off. "No bark! Go back to sleep."

Molly, standing in the doorway of her room, rubs her eyes. "What's going on?"

"Nothing," the boss answers. "Doodle was barking. Probably just getting used to the sounds of a new neighborhood."

Molly nods and turns back into her room.

"No bark!" the boss commands again. And with that he also goes back to bed. But I sit in the living room for a long time, head tilted, ears forward, listening. Finally, when I don't hear any new sounds, I go back to my rug.

The next morning, Molly puts me out to pee, heading off the kitten who once again tries to run into the house. She's a persistent thing, I'll give her that. I head straight to the fence bordering the driveway. And I smell him. Definitely an intruder. The hair rises on my back, but I don't bark. Whoever was here is long gone. Along with the intruder's scent, I smell the varied odors that mingle in the trash bin—all the stuff that the boss and Molly throw into the house trash cans, and then take out to the larger one. If you ask me, humans can be overly concerned with trash disposal.

When Molly brings me back in, she fills a bowl with cereal, grabs the milk from the fridge, and sits down to eat, a book beside her bowl.

The boss comes out dressed in his work shirt. "Ready to do some work?" he asks me, holding my harness. If he has treats—and I can smell that he does—I am! I go over to him and he buckles on the harness. "Don't forget to pull the trash can to the curb," he calls to Molly.

"Okay," Molly says, not moving from the kitchen table. She has her head bowed over her book. She likes to read at breakfast and sometimes, like today, she reads long after she's finished eating. The milk still sits on the table along with her bowl.

"They could come at any time now," the boss persists. "We don't want to miss it."

"Okay," Molly sounds exasperated, but this time she gets up, puts the milk away, and goes to the door. But she barely makes it outside when she sticks her head back in, her face drained of color.

"Dad. *Dad!* You got to see this." She turns back outside.

The boss and I hurry to join her on the porch. She's staring at the driveway.

The trashcan lies sideways on the cement, the lid gaping open. Papers, cans, cardboard, and bits of food litter the driveway and yard, some of it on the strip of lawn, and some in the flower beds.

"Who could have done this?" Molly sounds near tears. I go to her side in case the intruder has returned, working my nose.

For a moment, the boss and Molly both stare open-mouthed at the scene.

"Who could have done this?" Molly repeats. And then, "Doodle heard them! That's why he barked last night!"

The boss glances at me. "He must have. And I told him he was hallucinating."

Of *course* I heard them. The nose, or in this case, the ears, never lie.

"But I turned on the light and looked out. I didn't see anything," he says, shaking his head in disbelief. He and Molly continue to stare at the yard, both looking stunned.

And then with a cry, the boss runs over to our van.

"This is insane," he says, suddenly angry. He bends down touching a tire that is flat against the concrete. "What the—" here he uses what he calls language, something he almost *never* does.

And then Annie's car comes down the street. She pulls a little way into the driveway, stops, stares, then backs out and parks along the curb.

She gets out and rushes over to us. "What happened?" Her eyes are wide.

"No idea," the boss says. "Except someone really doesn't like us. Look at the van. Two flat tires."

Annie's face colors as she stares at the van. "Good grief. Who would—?"

"Chris Dodds," Molly says. "I bet that's who."

"Or her deadbeat son," the boss says. "Wants to make us leave so they can have the house." He glances at his phone. "I'm going to have to call the clients." He shakes his head. "I've already rescheduled twice."

Annie puts a hand on his arm. "Take my car. We can deal with this. Molly and me. Right Molly?"

Molly nods weakly.

The boss bends down, inspecting one of the tires. "I can't tell if they just let the air out of the tires or if they damaged them."

"I'll call someone to come out and check." Annie holds out her keys. "Go ahead and go. You don't want your customers to think you're a flake."

Reluctantly, he closes his fingers over them. "Okay," he says. But he doesn't sound okay. He sounds and smells angry. He goes back inside. Annie has the trashcan upright and she and Molly are already putting stuff inside by the time he returns with my leash and his bag and we go to her car.

Have I mentioned Annie's car is small? I take up the full length of the back seat and my head almost touches the ceiling.

"What an adventure, eh, Doodle?" the boss says, turning the key in the ignition. Not a good one, judging by the grim tone in his voice. The boss, tight-jawed and stiff-shouldered, pulls away. Through the window I watch Annie and Molly stooping to pick up trash.

Our first job is one of our regulars, a nursing home far enough from us that I have time to take a nap. The boss and I like the manager very much, a round, curly-haired Latina who is almost as old as many of her residents. She always tells us that we're well worth the money because if she ever got an infestation it would be a nightmare to treat.

"All those beds!" she likes to say. Plus, she gives me treats, and very nice ones at that. With the boss's permission, of course. The first time we searched her place, she asked the boss if I could visit some of the residents after we were done, because it always cheers them up to pet dogs. After that, it became part of our routine. So today I do the search, and then, as usual, visit a fair number of the patients, who ooh and aah over me, smiling and laughing. It always feels good to see them.

We finish, and are walking back to Annie's tiny car, when the boss's phone buzzes.

It's Annie. "I got Don's 24-Hour Repair to come by," she says. "I've used them before. They pumped up the tires and there are no leaks."

"Well, that's a relief," the boss says.

"And we got all trash picked up before the garbage truck came," she adds.

"Wonderful!" The muscles in the boss's jaw relax a little. They talk some more, and then we're off to our next job, also a regular, a motel chain out by a busy highway.

This manager, a tall, morose-faced man with an accent that the boss says is Indian, never has much to say to us. We search the lobby and all the rooms except for a couple that are still occupied. No bugs.

The boss stops for a hamburger after that, but uncharacteristically, doesn't finish it. Even more uncharacteristically, he hands me the unfinished portion of his burger. I swallow it quickly before he changes his mind. "What's going on, Doodle?" he asks, his voice thick with emotion.

Naturally, I can't answer but it must be something important if he can't finish his burger.

Our last job is on the way back, another motel chain and also a regular. The manager is a pinch-faced woman who looks stressed, but other than a quick nod and calling a maid to let us into the rooms, she has no contact with us. This motel takes pets and I encounter the scents of many different dogs and a couple of cats. None of the rooms has bed bugs, but a couple have fleas, not uncommon in pet-friendly motels, I've found. I don't alert on them because I'm not supposed to.

And then, we head home and find the driveway swept clean and the trashcan back against the fence. Everything back to normal. The boss lets me out and I stretch, glad to have more space. I have to say my crate in our van is much roomier.

When we get inside, the living room has changed. Most of the boxes are now against the walls. The couch, chair, and coffee table are empty.

The boss, looking amazed, says, "Wow! Did you hire a crew of elves to help while we were gone?"

Molly and Annie high five, grinning at each other. "Woman power!" Annie says. "We worked hard! But we're tired," she admits. "We ordered pizza for dinner. Be here in about half an hour."

"Sounds great to me," the boss says.

Sounds great to me also, but I don't hold much hope of getting any.

Hey! My bed is on the floor near the couch. I hurry over to it, sniffing it thoroughly to make sure nothing has changed. And then I lie down.

"Let's get that harness off first," the boss says, calling me to him. He unbuckles it, which frankly is a relief. I shake off the memory of the straps and go back to my bed, just to make sure it's still soft.

"I guess Doodle's glad to have his bed back," Molly says. "Oh, and guess what, Dad?"

The boss looks up.

"Marmie called me and said that they just got a new computer, and I could borrow their old laptop while I'm at Mom's. They'll bring it when they come up." Molly flashes him another big grin. "Marmie said you called and asked!"

Marmie and GrandJum are Molly's grandparents. They live in this great place with lots of trees called the Blue Ridge Mountains.

Now the boss's face splits into a smile. "That's wonderful!"

After a bit, I go to the mudroom door. I haven't had a pee in some time, plus I need to check the yard for intruders.

Molly comes over to let me out. But when she opens it, Moxy slips by her, darting inside and racing through the kitchen.

"Moxy!" Molly shouts, following her. "She wants to be a housecat," Molly says, as she comes back with the kitten in her arms.

"Not in the cards," the boss says.

Molly carries the cat into the mudroom, shutting the door to the kitchen firmly behind her. We all go out to the yard, Molly still holding the kitten. I've got my nose to the ground as soon as we're outside. I check the entire yard. I can catch only the stale, now very faint, scent of the intruder from the night before.

Molly sits on a lawn chair and pets the kitten.

Before long, I hear a car pull into the driveway. I bark. Not more intruders, I hope.

"The pizza's here," Molly announces. She puts the kitten down and we hurry back into the kitchen, where the delicious scent of cheese and pepperoni fill my nose. I lie down by Molly's feet.

They're just finishing dinner when Molly's phone bursts into its little melody that means she has a call. She jumps at the sound, then, looking chagrined, pulls it from her pocket and walks into the living room.

"Hey, Mom." Her voice is tight.

Cori's voice sounds a little tense as well. As usual, I have no idea what's going on, but tension between Molly and her mother is nothing new.

"If we're still invited," Cori says, "Benita and I would love to come to the wedding. I'm sorry I took so long to answer, but—"

"That's great!" All Molly's tension seems to have evaporated.

"Armando and Mariela aren't going to come. They wish they could, but summer is their busy season and they just don't feel they can take the time off."

Armando, one of Molly's Mexican relatives, owns this great restaurant in the Blue Ridge Mountains.

"That's okay. I really didn't expect them. I'm glad you're going to come." Molly beams at her phone screen.

"It'll be a very modern wedding," Cori says in a dry voice. "With the ex-spouse included."

"It'll be great. Annie . . . hoped you'd come." She glances at the boss and Annie who are both standing in the kitchen doorway listening with unabashed interest. Her face colors. "Dad, too," she adds quickly, the coloring deepening.

"Anyway, gotta run. Sorry to be slow to answer. This week's been a mess with work and stuff, and then, well . . ."

"No, don't worry. That's great," Molly says, once again. She seems to be at a loss for words. She says goodbye and puts the phone back in her pocket.

"They're coming," she says to the boss and Annie.

"Good!" Annie gives her a bright somewhat artificial smile. "We will try to make them as comfortable as possible."

"I should have told her what happened last night," Molly says. "Maybe she could have taken fingerprints or something."

"Not her jurisdiction," the boss says.

"Yeah. And she was in a hurry."

Molly's mother often seems to be in a hurry.

"But I'm still going to ask her about Kirby Banes. He might have a record or something, and if so, maybe Jordan's mom could get her money back."

Neither the boss nor Annie look hopeful about this. But Molly is much more cheerful as she goes into the kitchen to help clean up.

And I'm hopeful as well, because there are several crusts from the pizza still on her plate.

Chapter 10

Good and Bad Encounters

Right after breakfast, Molly clicks my walk collar around my neck, pockets her phone, and goes into the boss's bedroom. "Do you know where the extra collar and the Gentle Leader are? That Annie left for Cooper?"

The boss pauses, cord in hand. He's setting up his computer on his desk which is no longer stacked with boxes. "On the shelf by the mudroom door, I think. We're going to let that be for pet stuff."

Molly goes into the kitchen and comes back with the collars in hand. "We'll be back in about an hour."

"Jordan's mom will be there, right?"

"Yeah. I'm going to give Jordan a few training tips, and we'll take a walk with Cooper so he learns to relax when another dog is around."

"Okay," he says, bending to insert the plug into this multi-cord thing on the floor.

It's still cool when we go outside, with a slight grass-scented breeze that for once isn't overpowered by the smell of gas or asphalt.

We find Jordan waiting for us on his porch, Cooper on a leash beside him.

Cooper, of course, goes berserk when he sees us, barking and pulling and jumping. Jordan keeps a firm grip on the leash, but although it's cool, he has beads of sweat on his forehead.

Molly takes me over to a shady spot along the backyard fence and ties my leash to a post. "Down!" she commands. I lie down. "Stay." I settle in the grass, filling my nose with grass and earth scents.

She goes over to Jordan, who is watching her, his face filled with amazement. "I wish Cooper would do that," he says. He's holding Cooper on a tight, close leash. Cooper tries to lunge as Molly comes up to him, but Jordan holds him back.

"He can. It's not magic. It's hard work, time, and patience. At least that's what Annie says." Molly looks down at Cooper. "Of course, she also says some dogs are harder than others, but—" she bends down to stroke Cooper under the chin "—you're not going to be one of those, are you, Cooper?"

Cooper licks her hand. She laughs. "He may not be much of a service dog, but he's nice."

She holds up the collar she brought. "This is like the one Annie put on him when she came over. It's a martingale collar," she says, holding it up. "It tightens when he pulls but won't hurt his throat like a choke collar. It's good, too, because it's really hard for a dog to slip out of it and run away. Can you put it on him?"

Jordan does, with some effort because Cooper wriggles around trying to see what's going on.

"It fits," Molly says happily after inserting her fingers between the collar and Cooper's neck. "Annie said it would. She's good at that." Molly pulls out the ring of the collar. "Switch the leash to this one," she says to Jordan, who does so.

I hear the front door creak. Keira comes out and stands on the porch, watching.

Molly takes the leash and relaxes it. The second Cooper starts to pull she gives a little jerk. "No," she says in a firm voice. "Sit." Cooper looks confused for a second, but then sits. "*Good* boy," Molly says. She gives him a treat and strokes him under the chin. He pops back up again, and she repeats the sit command, praising him when he is calm. Or calmer. There is nothing in Cooper's personality that is truly calm.

"You're great!" Keira says.

Molly flushes. "Thanks. Annie taught me."

"Yeah, she's terrific," Keira says. "Had Cooper eating out of her hand in no time." Her voice turns bitter. "Not that we should have to be doing this with a $15,000 dog. Did Jordan tell you? Every time we call Life Support Assistance Dogs they tell us they haven't found out anything. And this last time, Lisa, that manager, the one I thought was so nice? She tells me they're investigating it, but I need to quit calling them. They'll let me know when they find out something." She flashes an angry glance at Molly. "Don't call us. We'll call you." She shakes her head. "You'd think they'd care more about their reputation."

Molly says, "That's weird." She looks thoughtful. "Have you heard of Madison Greene?"

Keira shakes her head.

"The Low Down News?"

"Oh, yeah. That vlogging thing? I haven't listened to it, but a friend at work loves it."

"Madison, the one who does it, is the mom of a good friend of mine. I could give you her number. She's really good at putting pressure on people when they stonewall you."

"Really?" Keira asks, a sliver of hope in her voice.

"Yeah. I think she would help if I asked her. I sometimes sell her my photos. And she's always interested in dog stories because she says they get lots of hits. I'll text Grady—her son—when I get home and ask him. Do you happen to have a photo of Banes? That would help."

Keira shakes her head. "I tried to take one of him and Cooper when he first brought him over, and he almost got angry about it." She grimaces. "That should have been a red flag. I can't believe I was taken in by that man."

Jordan, looking a little embarrassed, says, "I have one. I took it when he wasn't looking. One of him and Cooper."

Both Molly and Keira stare at him a second. Then his mother touches his shoulder. "To the rescue!"

"That'd be great," Molly says. "It could really help. If you send it to me, I'll forward it to Grady and have him tell his mom about what's happened."

"Thanks!" Keira looks less angry now. "And I have an appointment with legal aid to see if they can help in any way."

Molly nods. Then with a glance downward, she tilts her head at Jordan, "Look who's lying at my feet all calm."

Jordan gives her a smile. "For the moment."

"Should we try a walk?" Molly hands the leash to Jordan and comes over to untie me. "You start off with him and I'll catch up to you. If he tries to lunge at us, give him a correction just like Annie taught you."

Jordan and Cooper start walking toward the road. Soon we catch up to them, me walking calmly beside Molly like the Canine Good Citizen that I am. Cooper is not particularly calm, but with Jordan's corrections the leash is loose much of the time. Well, at least part of the time. We walk to the end of the street and turn at the first side road. This one has fewer homes and more apartment buildings. As we come up to a medium-sized brick one, Molly suddenly slows down.

"What?" Jordan stops a little ahead of her, correcting Cooper as he tries to keep going.

"See that woman by that blue hatchback?"

Jordan looks to where Molly is pointing. Two people are getting out of a car, a younger man with his hair pulled back into a ponytail, and an older woman who looks familiar. "Yeah?"

"Chris Dodds," Molly says in a hushed voice. "She came by our place and told us we had to move out because Mrs. Thomas, our landlord, had promised she could have it."

"Really?" Jordan gives Molly a sharp look. "That's crazy. Why would she rent it to you then?"

The ponytail man starts toward the entrance of the building. The woman opens the car's back door and lifts out a couple of grocery bags.

"Exactly. And that's not all." Molly starts to say more but the woman stiffens, staring at Molly.

"Hey! You.!" The woman's voice is harsh. "You're that girl, right? In the Thomas place." She strides toward us, the bags swinging from her hands.

I recognize her now as I catch a whiff of her scent. The angry woman at the door! I edge forward, the hair rising on my back. Cooper tries to greet her, but Jordan holds the leash in a tight grip.

"Yeah." Molly's voice is tight and thin. And then, defiantly, "Our place now."

Chris Dodds glares at her. "We'll see. Did your dad call Mrs. Thomas?"

Molly straightens her shoulders and raises her head. I pull forward a little more, calm but on alert. "You know what? He did call her. And she told him she wanted us as her renters."

Chris Dodds makes a sound like she's clearing her throat.

Molly's face is pale, and her voice strained but she continues, "So quit trying to make us leave. Nothing you do will matter because we won't be forced out. And my mom's a cop. So if you do that trash thing again, we're going to file a harassment charge."

"What are you talking about?" Chris Dodds steps closer.

"Spreading our trash all over the yard!" Molly glares back at her. "Making our tires flat."

I'm confused because the scent of this woman is not the scent on the trash can. That was a man.

"What?" Chris Dodds looks at her like she's crazy. "Are you joking?"

Jordan suddenly steps between Molly and the woman. "Leave her alone," he says in a firm tone.

"Yeah, like I'm going to listen to a punk like you!" Chris Dodds says. But she takes a step back.

"Mom!" the ponytailed man calls from the doorway of the apartment building, his whiny voice dragging out the word. "I didn't bring my key."

Chris Dodds waves a hand in his direction. "Coming."

Cooper seems to finally get the idea that this is not a friendly encounter and growls. Jordan pulls the leash even tighter and says, "No!"

Chris Dodds gives Cooper a sour look. She turns back to Molly and Jordan. "Better watch those dogs. I see them running around here, I'm calling animal control." With that she turns and clomps toward the ponytail man at the entrance.

Molly watches her go. I can feel her hand trembling on the leash.

"Wow. Crazy mean," Jordan says. "What were you talking about with the trash?"

Molly tells him about the trash can being emptied all over our yard and the flat tires.

"Crazy mean," Jordan repeats, shaking his head. "I wish my dad—" he blinks hard.

Molly starts walking, and soon we're side by side as we were before.

"I'm sorry about your dad," Molly says in a soft voice.

"Yeah." Jordan's voice can barely be heard. "He hated bullies. He would have put that woman in her place in a hot minute."

We turn at the next corner, neither Molly nor Jordan talking. Finally Jordan says, "Your mom is a cop? That's cool!"

"A detective, actually." Molly gives him a crooked smile. "In Alexandria. This isn't her jurisdiction, but that woman doesn't have to know that."

"I wish she was in Manassas. Then she could investigate Kirby Banes. And Life Support."

For a few moments, the only sound is of our footsteps. When we reach the next corner and turn back on Jordan's street, Molly says, "Sometimes my mom knows police officers in other areas that she can ask to check things. I could ask her about Life Support and Kirby Banes.

"That'd be great." Jordan says. "Really great."

When we get back to Jordan's, he trades the new collar for Cooper's old one. "Thanks for bringing this," he says, holding it out.

"Annie says you can keep it. You can use it anytime you walk him or are with him on leash. Just don't leave it on him if he's by himself. He could maybe catch the chain on something."

Jordan nods, and we head back to our place.

When we get home, Molly puts me in the backyard for a bit. I check the fence line and make sure there have been no intruders and I pee in a few places just to make sure our boundaries will be known to anything with a decent nose. Humans aren't included in that group. Then I give my usual single bark, asking to come in. Molly, on the phone, opens the mudroom door, and then deftly toes the kitten from the doorway while I go inside.

"Okay," she says. "See you." She goes into the boss's bedroom. He's unpacking books and placing them on one of the bookshelves we brought from the other place.

"Dad, is it okay if Grady comes over? And Snippet?"

Grady is Molly's good friend. Not as good as Tanya, but almost. He goes to her school but is a grade ahead because he's older. We've had lots of adventures with Grady, some of them a little scary to be honest. Luckily, everything's fine now.

The boss frowns and rubs a hand across his forehead which comes away damp, and then selects another book. "For how long?" he asks without looking up. "We've got so much to do before the wedding. Only three more days."

"Just for like an hour or so. He wanted to see the house."

"And he needs Snippet for that?"

"Well . . ."

The boss turns from the bookshelf to gaze at Molly with sudden attention. "Well what?"

"Well, I was telling him about Moxy, and he really wants to get a cat, but Madison says he doesn't even know if Snippet likes cats. So he asked if he could bring her over and see how she acts around Moxy."

Madison is Grady's mother. We've had some scary adventures with her as well, come to think of it.

The boss's frown deepens. "Not sure what Moxy will think about that!"

"We'll be careful. He'll keep Snippet on leash. And she's really good about obeying him. And we'll do it in the backyard so if Moxy gets scared she can escape into the mudroom."

"Just him, not Madison, right?"

Molly nods.

"Because I don't have time for visiting," the boss says.

"Especially Madison," Molly says with a knowing look. Not sure why, but the boss says Madison is a natural flirt and he doesn't like it when she flirts with him. This goes back to when they first met, and they had a kind of falling out.

But Molly likes her better than the boss and sometimes sells her photos.

The boss's eyes go back to the boxes of books near the shelf. "I guess. But not over an hour. Everyone will be coming into town tomorrow and we've got—" he waves a hand at room.

"—so much to do," Molly finishes for him. "I know. I'm almost done with my room and with the stuff I have to put away in the kitchen."

"Good," the boss says, his attention now firmly on the book in his hand.

"Thanks!" Molly goes back to unpacking in her room and I settle down on the rug.

When I hear Madison's van, I run to the door, but don't bark because I know who it is.

Molly nudges me aside to open the door. She waves at Madison and waits for Grady and Snippet to come inside.

Grady is a stocky guy, quite a bit taller than Molly, with short hair that's straight up in the front. He has on sandals, shorts, and his usual T-shirt with a zombie on it. Grady's a big fan of zombie movies. Snippet, as I might have mentioned, is this Irish setter Golden mix who is incredibly fast at fly ball.

Snippet and I greet each other calmly, like the Canine Good Citizens we both are.

"Hey, this is nice." Grady gives the room an appreciative glance. "Lots more space."

"Yeah, my room is almost twice as big," Molly says.

The doorbell rings. I give a low woof in surprise.

Molly looks surprised too, and then a little dismayed when she opens the door.

Madison wafts in, a cloud of perfumy scent clinging to her. Almost as tall as the boss, Madison usually is dressed up in pointy heels, slacks, and a billowy blouse. Today, though, she's wearing shorts and a T-shirt and sandals that show her lacquered toenails. I give them a discreet sniff.

"I decided I just absolutely had to see your new place," she says, pushing back a strand of her long hair. "Since I'm already right here." She gives Molly a bright smile.

"Sure," Molly says, with an anxious glance toward the boss's bedroom.

Molly takes her and Grady on a short tour of the house. Snippet and I exchange a few more sniffs as we follow along, catching up on where we've been.

"It's not new like your place," Molly says. Grady lives in a fancy home that full of shiny tile and shiny wood floors. It has a pretty big yard, too, but all the trees are tiny.

"But this is nice sized," Madison responds. "And charming in its own way."

Molly leads us to her bedroom and then to the bathroom.

"Huge bathroom," Grady says, as we move on.

"But only one. You have three, right?"

"Three and a half," he admits.

Finally, Molly takes us to the boss's room.

Madison smiles at him and says, "I do believe you're just about swallowed whole in boxes!"

"Tell me!" the boss half-groans, greeting her and Grady with a small wave.

"You should see what it was a few days ago!" Molly says. "Practically wall to wall."

"Well, you have a prize here. A lovely place. And congratulations on the wedding," Madison says briskly. "I see you have your work cut out for you, so I won't stand in your way."

She leaves after that, telling Grady she'll be back in an hour.

"So, we'll do the cat thing in the backyard?" he asks.

Molly nods. "That way Moxy has an escape if she's too scared." She explains about the cat door in the mudroom.

"Thanks for doing this!" Grady says. "Mama keeps saying that before we can consider getting a cat we have to know that Snippet won't eat it."

This surprises me. While dogs aren't especially fond of cats, I haven't personally met any who eat them. Coyotes maybe. I've heard stories. But cat on the menu doesn't sound good to me. Give me liver treats any day.

"Got a good grip?" Molly asks. She grabs her camera and slings the strap over her shoulder.

Grady tightens the leash. "Yeah."

She opens the door to the mudroom. Moxy's face peers through the crack as Molly opens the door. Lately, she's always there, ready to try to run in. But this time, she sees Snippet and with a yowl rockets straight up and somehow veers over to her shelf. Gotta give cats credit—they can really jump when they want to.

Snippet lunges forward, interested, but doesn't growl or bark, and after a firm, "No pull!" from Grady relaxes the tension on the leash.

"This is a great yard!" he says, when we step outside. "Bigger than ours!"

Molly nods. "Yeah. Dad says it's like sitting on an oil field or gold mine because all the real estate people want to buy this place and put apartments on it."

"Mama said she paid a fortune for our place just because it had a decent-sized yard," Gray says, agreeing.

"Should we let them run around a bit first?" Molly asks, glancing down at me.

"Sure. Drain some of her energy." Grady unclips Snippet's leash. She immediately bows and I bow back, and soon we're racing around the yard full speed.

Molly and Grady sit in the plastic lawn chairs under the trees. From the bits of conversation I hear as we fly past, she's telling him about Jordan and Kirby Banes.

After a while, Grady calls Snippet back to him. We collapse under the tree, panting as we lie beside his and Molly's feet.

"I could help," Grady is saying. "Mama has a couple of search accounts because of her vlog. Maybe he'll turn up there."

I see a motion over by the house. Moxy! She slinks through the cat door and then sits and watches us before creeping closer.

Molly says in a low voice, "Guess who's out of the mudroom."

Grady glances up and leans down to attach Snippet's leash. But he's too late. Snippet goes rigid and then bolts toward the kitten at a dead run.

"Snippet!" Grady yells, tearing after her. "Come!"

Snippet usually obeys, but this time she doesn't seem to hear him.

Moxy dashes back through the cat door. Snippet skids to a stop in front of it, sniffing, her tail waving wildly. Grady is just catching up to her when Moxy sticks her head out the door, hisses, and swipes Snippet on the nose.

With a yelp, Snippet jumps back.

That's the thing about cats. They have these incredibly sharp claws and you never know when they'll use them.

Grady grabs Snippet's collar, attaches the leash, and leads a now chagrined Snippet back under the tree.

"Well, that didn't go as planned. I shouldn't have taken her off leash." He sounds bitter.

Molly, though, is laughing. "Moxy's okay. And I think Snippet just learned a valuable lesson about cats."

You think? Unpredictable defines cats. And unpredictable combined with claws like knives? Dangerous!

But Grady, his face glum, says, "So much for that idea."

Molly stands up. "They haven't been introduced yet. Wait here. Keep a tight grip on the leash." She starts for the mudroom door. "Come on, Doodle."

I join her and when we get to the cat door, Molly calls, "Here, kitty-kitty." Pretty soon a head pops through the opening. And then, after a cautious look around the yard, Moxy slips out and rubs against Molly, purring. Then she twines around my legs. Over by the tree, Snippet sits watching us intently. But she doesn't bark or growl. She's just very *very* interested.

Molly picks up Moxy. "Let's go meet a new friend." She carries the kitten back to the tree, slowing as we approach Grady and Snippet.

Moxy, of course, tenses up. That's the other thing about cats. They're such nervous creatures, seeing danger everywhere.

"Relax," Molly says, petting her.

Snippet is interested, but cautious. Remembering the swipe on her nose, I bet. She sits in an alert position, sniffing for all she's worth, but not moving closer to the kitten.

After a bit, Moxy relaxes in Molly's arms. "See?" she says. "They're doing well." She goes over and sits down in the lawn chair, still holding the kitten. I lie down at her feet. Snippet leans forward, whining softly, still sniffing, but not getting within paw range. Moxy regards her, sniffing some herself.

Molly pets Moxy, and then reaches out with one hand and pets Snippet.

"Keep a tight grip," she says again to Grady.

She gently puts Moxy down, who retreats under her chair.

Moxy stays under the chair for some time while Molly and Grady talk about Kirby Banes. Snippet lies down, her eyes on the kitten.

And then, ever so cautiously, Moxy edges out from under the chair, her gaze fixed on Snippet, who watches without moving. Molly is holding her breath and I think Grady is, too.

Slowly, slowly, with several jumps backward, Moxy touches Snippet's nose. Snippet doesn't move except to sniff. Both Molly and Grady let out their breath.

Moxy jumps back but comes forward again when Snippet doesn't follow. More nose touching. More jumping back. But then Moxy comes forward and rubs against Snippet, purring. Snippet sends a questioning glance to Grady, who says in a soft voice, "Good girl."

Molly raises her camera and clicks it a couple of times. 'Here's the proof," she says, leaning over to show Grady. You have to give Moxy credit. She's pretty brave. First Doodle and now Snippet! Only Chloe to go."

Brave? Maybe. But I can see by Snippet's body language that she doesn't mean to hurt her, and I think Moxy can too.

Grady's phone beeps. "Mama," he says, glancing at his screen. "Gotta go."

We all head back into the house, all of us except a very unhappy Moxy, that is. We leave her yowling in the mudroom.

And then we hear a honk, and Grady and Snippet are out the door, with Molly calling after him, "Don't forget to check on Kirby Banes."

Chapter 11

Packing It All Up

It is the day before the wedding and everyone in the house is as excited as a pack of dogs about to go on a walk. Maybe more. Grandjum and Marmie, Molly's grandparents, are sitting at the kitchen table listening to Molly tell them about my part in the wedding.

"I think Doodle will do himself proud," Marmie says taking a sip of her coffee. A plump woman with alert dark eyes, she's always been one of those people, like Reverend Henry, who radiates calmness—which is quite a feat given the current atmosphere.

"Mom and I will come back here and pick up Doodle after the reception," Molly says. "And I'll come by every day to feed Moxy and give her some attention."

Marmie gives Molly a wistful glance. "I wish you could have come and stayed with us while Josh and Annie are gone. We would have been happy to bring you home after they get back."

"I know," Molly says, apologetically. "That would have been fun. But there'd be no one to watch the kitten. And Dad says boarding is expensive."

Grandjum, who looks like an older, beardless version of the boss, says, "I wonder how long it will take before that little sprite becomes a housecat."

"Dad says never," Molly replies.

Grandjum leans back in his chair looking amused. "We'll see. Your dad's bark is worse than his bite."

What? To my knowledge the boss never barks.

"Just like his daddy," Marmie says, with a fond glance at her husband.

Now I'm totally confused.

GrandJum rubs his chin—reminding me of the boss rubbing his beard. "What time is Doodle's appointment?"

Molly glances up at the clock. "At eight-thirty. We've got a few minutes."

"There might be traffic," GrandJum says sounding *exactly* like the boss. He gets the keys and Molly loads me into my crate.

"You're going to get groomed and look perfect for the wedding tomorrow," she tells me.

"And smell perfect," Marmie adds, although I don't know why. I smell much better right now than I will after Mrs. Yashimoto adds that flowery scent to my fur. I always have to roll in the grass to rub it off first chance I get.

When we get to the groomer's, Molly and Marmie take me inside while GrandJum waits in the van. Before long, Mrs. Yashimoto walks briskly over to us.

"Good morning, Mr. Doodle," she says, stroking me under the chin.

She's a thin, birdlike woman, so tiny that boss has said more than once that he thinks I might weigh more than she does. "A strong wind could blow her away," he likes to say. But he's wrong. She's surprisingly strong, and her hands are steady and sure. Except for getting the hair out of my ears, she never hurts me, and she always apologizes during that part and gives me good treats. "So so sorry, Mr. Doodle," she always says in her calm voice, "but if we don't do this, you might get an ear infection." I have my doubts. Humans always think they know what's good for dogs, but are so often clueless. But that's the only bad part, and, as I said, she has excellent treats.

Even though I don't particularly like getting groomed, especially getting the hair pulled out of my ears, I like Mrs. Yashimoto very much. She waves at Molly and Marmie and leads me to her station in the back of the store.

By the time Mrs. Yashimoto brings me back out to the lobby, my hair is shorter, brushed soft and fluffy, my inner ears are hairless, and my nails have been trimmed. The only bad thing (other than the ears) is that I now smell like lavender, which, take it from me, is not a scent any self-respecting dog wants to have.

"Doodle, you look great!" Molly says, when she sees me.

Mrs. Yashimoto smiles down at me. "You're all ready for the wedding now, aren't you, Mr. Doodle?"

Molly hands her a tip, something the boss always does. "Dad said to thank you again for working him in," she says.

"Thank you very much. Always a pleasure to spend time with Mr. Doodle." She pockets the money and gives me a final pat on the back.

Molly and I go over to Marmie, who is putting a receipt in her purse.

"He smells much better!" Marmie exclaims.

As I said, humans are clueless.

Molly suddenly sucks in her breath and goes stiff. Her eyes are on a man leading a young black Labrador retriever over to Mrs. Yashimoto. The man looks about the age of the boss, but a little taller, heavier, and clean-shaven. He's wearing jeans that are much tighter than the boss wears, and a T-shirt with some writing on it.

"It's him," Molly says under her breath.

No idea what she means. I've never met this man before. At least, I don't recognize his face. Too many dogs and people in the room to be sure of his particular scent from this distance, plus my nose is clogged with lavender.

But Molly seems to recognize him. She whips out her phone and takes several photos, flipping it closed with a guilty expression when he turns and glances in our direction. The man doesn't appear to notice.

Marmie, at the door, turns to Molly. "Ready?" Molly hurries to catch up. I can smell the tension on Molly now, even through the lavender, and after she puts me in my crate, she sits stiff as a pole behind me in the back seat the whole way home.

She takes me straight to the backyard when we get home, pulling out her phone as she goes to stand under the tree.

"Tanya!" Molly's voice is thick with excitement. Guess who I saw? At the groomers?" Without waiting for a response, she says, "Kirby Banes!"

It takes Tanya a moment to respond. "The fake service dog guy?"

"Yeah! He gave Mrs. Yashimoto—that's Doodle's groomer—a dog to groom."

"Are you sure it was him?"

"Pretty sure. I have that photo from Celia and the one from Jordan. And I'm going to call Mrs. Yashimoto and see what she says." Molly sighs. "And then try not worry about it until after the wedding."

"It's going to be so cool," Tanya says. "Mama got my dress cleaned. Tonight, we can we wear anything, right?"

"Yeah. It's just to make sure we know where to stand and stuff." She and Tanya start talking about the wedding while I make one last round of the yard's perimeter. No unusual scents, I'm happy to say, which does not mean that there are no cat scents, because there are *always* cat scents, just no new ones.

When we go back inside, Molly goes to her computer. "Here's Celia's photo," she says, frowning at the screen which shows a darkish image of a man. "Pretty blurry. But—" she clicks some keys and another image appears "—Jordan's is clearer. And I'm sure it's the same man I saw. At least I think I'm sure."

She clicks more keys, stares at the screen for a bit, and then taps her phone.

"Mrs. Yashimoto?" Molly asks, when a voice says, "Good afternoon."

"It's Molly Hunter. Doodle's owner."

"Yes, Molly." Mrs. Yashimoto sounds surprised. "Was there something wrong with Doodle's groom?"

"No. He's perfect like always. I . . . I um have a question for you, though. When we were leaving, I saw you with your next grooming, er, um, client."

"Yes, the usual bath and brush," she says.

"Could you tell me his name?"

A long pause.

Molly says, "I wouldn't ask, but well—" She plunges into the story, telling Mrs. Yashimoto about Jordan and Cooper and how the man she saw looked like the photos she has.

"Ah. Yes." Mrs. Yashimoto is silent for a long time. "I don't like to give any information on my clients. But to cheat a boy and his mother . . ." Another pause. "Will you promise me one thing?" she asks.

"Yes! I mean, what?"

"This man, if he turns out not to be the one you're looking for, you won't tell anyone about him. Or that I gave you his name?"

"Yes! I promise!" Molly adds with some emotion, "I wouldn't ever want to get you in trouble."

Mrs. Yashimoto sighs. "His name is Dyson Banks. He has been a client for a few years, but he almost always brings a different dog. He told me he's a scout to find dogs that would make good service dogs."

"Really!" Molly's voice jumps higher. "Service dogs!"

"That is why I decided to tell you," Mrs. Yashimoto says. "This man has never left a good impression on me—too smooth if you know what I mean."

"But the name is what? *Dyson* Banes?"

"Dyson Banks. With a k."

"Okay." Molly frowns. "Not the same name, but I'm going to check it out. And if it's not the same guy, I won't tell anyone anything."

"One more thing." Mrs. Yashimoto hesitates for a second. "He asked the shop owners for a discount because he's trying to find good service dogs. They asked me if I'd reduce my normal rate."

"Did you?" Molly asks.

"I might have. But this Mr. Banks, he dresses very nicely. Expensive clothes. And expensive car—I saw him once loading one of his dogs after a groom. I figured if the service dog people needed money, *he* could give it to them. I have a tight budget.

Also," she says, her voice dry and I can almost see the smile on her face, "he never tips."

"Wow," Molly says. "Thank you so much. I really appreciate it."

"This man, if he turns out to be a fraud, will you let me know?"

"Yes, definitely. I'll let you know as soon as we do—whether he's the one or not."

With that, they say goodbye. Molly stares at her computer screen for a moment. Then, she opens her phone again.

"Grady?" she says, when Grady's voice comes over the line.

"Hey. I didn't have time to do too much searching, but I found some stuff. First, I can't find anything on Kirby Banes. So I have to wonder if he's using an alias. Usually when I search a name, I'll find lots of people with the same name, all over the country. But I don't even get that. Just schools and places. So that's weird."

Molly says, "Not so weird after all." She explains about seeing the man at the groomer's and her call to Mrs. Yashimoto. "So I think—"

"—he's using an alias!" Grady says. "Yeah, I'll check it out. What's the name?"

Molly gives it to him and then says, "And I have photos. I'll send them to you." And then, "Got to go. We have a rehearsal tonight and I still have to finish packing my stuff and Doodle's to go to Mom's after the wedding."

"I'll let you know what I find tomorrow," Grady says, "if you're not too busy." They say goodbye and Molly starts to pack. As always, she has trouble deciding what to take to her mom's, so she spends a long time with that, and then she has to do computer stuff on the laptop she's borrowing from Marmie and GrandJum. I nap. When I wake up, she's got her suitcase ready to go, along with her pillow and two tote bags.

If humans followed the example of dogs when it comes to packing, there'd be a lot less unpacking for them to do. Except for my kibble, which Molly places by the front door, everything of mine fits in a single plastic grocery bag. Just sayin'. . .

After a bit, I hear a knock and then Annie sticks her head in the door. "Hello," she calls.

"They're here!" Molly shouts, and leads me outside, with the boss and Marmie and GrandJum following.

Hey. Annie's not alone. She has two women sitting in her tiny car, a gray-haired woman in the front, and a younger one who looks about Annie's age in the back. And Chloe.

Everyone crowds around her car, talking and laughing with the two women. Turns out the older one is Annie's mother, and the younger one her sister. Both of them live in New York, a place I've heard of but never been to.

We get in our van and after stopping to pick up Tanya, we go to the church, where the parking lot already is half full.

Matt, the boss's brother, is here. According to the boss, he's the best man—best at what, I have no idea. If GrandJum looks like an older, beardless version of the boss, Matt looks like a taller, heavier version of them both. He has closely cut hair, thinning on top, and muscular arms, one of them tattooed.

He and the boss hug—getting married seems to involve lots of hugging—and talk a little about work. The boss introduces him to Annie and her family and asks about his wife and kids.

"All doing great," Matt says. "They'll be here for the wedding, of course. They're eager to see Doodle." He smiles down at me.

We all wait outside until Reverend Henry sticks his head out the door and waves for us to come in.

Reverend Henry says, "Now, the organist will be playing and when Mrs. Henry here—" he gestures at the slight, gray-haired woman standing beside him "—gives you the signal, you'll line up, side by side."

Mrs. Henry gives us a big smile. "You're going to be the highlight of the wedding!"

"I hope in a good way," Tanya murmurs.

Annie says, "Molly, you take the left side, and have Doodle on your left by the pews. Tanya, you'll be by the pews on the right side, with Chloe heeling on your left. I've organized a few distractions for the dogs, because there are always distractions in these kinds of events."

We all get into position. The organ starts to play. Mrs. Henry nods at Molly. "Now," she says.

"Try to keep time with the music," Mrs. Henry says, "but take small steps and go slowly."

A regular walking pace for a human is slow for a dog, but this is even slower. I bet a turtle could walk faster. Maybe a beetle. It's hard not to get ahead, and once Molly whispers, "no pull" and I have to wait for her to catch up.

We're about halfway down the length of the church, when Marmie suddenly claps and yells, "Go, Doodle!"

I start to turn toward her, but Molly says, "Heel!" in a low voice, so I continue to heel. A Canine Good Citizen ignores distractions as does a certified bed bug dog. A little further on, GrandJum tosses a ball into the aisle. No idea what's going on, but Chloe and I continue to heel until at long last we make it up to the front. Molly leads me to stand by the boss, and Tanya leads Chloe over to Annie.

"Good job!" Annie says, giving the girls a thumbs up. "Passed with flying colors."

Reverend Henry says, "Yes. Impressive. Very well-trained dogs. And now you'll wait there until they are ready for the rings." He talks some more, and Molly and Tanya act out giving something to the boss and Annie, even though neither of them has anything in their hands.

After that, the boss and Annie sit down in the front pew and Reverend Henry talks to them. We go back outside under a tree to wait. If weddings involve lots of hugging, which obviously they do, they also involve lots of waiting. To top things off, when we finally pack up in the van and go home, I learn that all the humans are going to leave again. Something about a rehearsal dinner. They have to practice eating dinner too? It boggles the mind.

Molly puts Chloe and me in the backyard before she leaves, taking time to check the lock on the gate that the boss installed after the trash can incident. "Just in case someone gets ideas," he said at the time. Mysterious as always.

"You two be good!" Molly says before leaving.

Chloe and I play a few games of chase, but it's pretty hot and muggy so we get big drinks and collapse under the trees. Moxy, still shy around Chloe, doesn't come out of the mudroom.

I stretch out, filling my nose with grass scent and listening to the typical night sounds—bird calls, a few buzzing insects, the occasional car coming down the street, snatches of conversation from nearby neighbors.

And then I hear a car pull up to the curb. One with a very quiet engine. Cars come and go all the time, so no big deal. Except then I hear a door close and footsteps approaching our house, coming up the driveway. Chloe hears it too and dashes to the fence with that baying bark beagles have. I add my voice to hers, and together we make quite a racket.

"Hush!" comes a harsh whisper. Something is tossed over the fence. I run to it, sniffing. A piece of meat. Chloe snatches it from under my nose and streaks back toward the tree. I follow her, but she gives me a warning look, growling slightly. Seriously? Anyway, I'm more interested in the man—because I can smell it's a man—standing on the other side of the fence. I bark to let him know he's intruding.

"Shut up!" he rasps, jiggling the latch. Then he curses in a soft but intense voice using a *lot* of language. Something about the lock.

And then I hear footsteps, a door slam, and the sound of the car driving away.

I bark some more in case he thinks of coming back. Chloe joins me, looking smug and smelling of beef.

Very odd. But I know his scent. It's a familiar one and I won't ever forget.

This is the man who scattered the trash.

Chapter 12

I Do! and No Way!

THE WEDDING IS A CONFUSION OF SCENTS, CONVERSAtions, preaching, walking down aisles, and music. Lots of hugging, lots of people talking in excited voices before it begins. Marmie and GrandJum, Matt and his family, Annie's sister and mother are here along with the Franklins, who pause on their way into the church to wish Tanya and Molly good luck and comment on how good we all look. Everyone is dressed up. I almost don't recognize Molly's mother when she walks by in a nice dress and sparkly sandals. And holy cow! Grady's wearing a suit! Who knew he even had one? And his straight-up hair is gelled and stiff. Madison, his mother, clicks by in very high heels, a tight dress, and a cloud of floral scent.

Despite a sharp tension flowing down the leash from Molly, our walk through the church goes perfectly. The same for Tanya and Chloe. No one shouts or throws a ball, but there are some chuckles and a few oohs and aahs as we do the procession. We sit beside Molly and Tanya like the Canine Good Citizens that we are, and watch when the rings are handed to Annie and the boss.

At one point, Tanya hands Chloe's leash to Molly and goes up to the front to sing. I'm no expert on music, not really too much a dog thing, but I know some is soothing and some is annoying. And I have to say I love listening to Tanya sing. It's both soothing and, I don't know, somehow deeply satisfying.

All like a smaller version of the other wedding I went to, only this one with people I know. The big surprise is when the boss does the part he practiced at home, what he calls the vows. Suddenly, tears well in his eyes and he is unable to speak. I wonder if I should go up to him and lick his hand even though we don't really have that kind of relationship. But then the leash trembles and Molly's eyes are watering, too. Not with sadness I realize. The emotion that flows from them both is what I can only describe as joy. Like a dog home again after a long hard journey, or a milk-mouthed puppy snuggling up to its mother.

And finally, after a few more words from Reverend Henry, who still smells a little like popcorn, he proclaims the boss and Annie to be husband and wife. They kiss and everyone cheers, and cameras flash, and then they go back down the aisle. We follow them through the big doors. And everyone else streams out to join us, clustering around the boss and Annie, congratulating them.

Almost everyone. Cori comes outside and stands in front of the church looking uncertain. Molly leads me over to her.

"Thanks for coming." Molly sounds shy now, hesitant. "I hope it wasn't too bad."

Cori shrugs. "Bittersweet, I'll admit." She swallows. "Memories, you know? But it was absolutely worth it to see you go down that aisle." She pulls Molly into a hug. "You are a beautiful girl."

Now Molly is teary all over again. "Thanks, Mom," she murmurs.

"Benita sends her apologies. She really wanted to see you but wasn't feeling well tonight."

"That's fine," Molly says. "Tell her I hope she feels better soon."

Then Cori, her old self again, releases Molly and says briskly, "Text me when you're ready to leave the reception and I'll get you and we can go pick up Doodle."

Molly nods. "I will. We're all packed."

"And . . ." another hesitation. "Will you give my congratulations to your Dad and Annie?"

Another nod. "Sure. They were really glad you came."

Molly stands and watches her mother leave, and then walks back to Tanya.

To my surprise, I see a familiar shape limping toward us from the church. Miguel, my old trainer! I'm surprised because Miguel hates crowds. He calls himself the last great loner. Not sure what that means except, well, he hates crowds. But here he is at a wedding. Not only that, he has a short, round woman walking beside him, hanging onto his arm. I don't know how I missed that he was in the church, but I did not catch his scent when we walked in.

Miguel is the one who rescued me from the animal shelter and trained me to be a bed bug dog. He is one of my all-time favorite people. All the dogs he trains love him. Quiet, firm, fair. Not given to lots of praise, but when he does give it, it means something, if you catch my drift. I start to go to him, tugging gently on the end of the leash.

"No pull," Molly says automatically. But then she looks in the same direction and calls, "Miguel!" To Tanya, she says, "That must be Rosa, his girlfriend."

Miguel has a girlfriend? The last great loner? What next? He's going to start training cats instead of dogs?

We go over to him and the woman, who is a Latina about the same age as Miguel with graying hair pulled back into a bun. She smiles, her round black eyes friendly and interested.

I greet Miguel calmly despite the fact that I'm excited to see him, because he expects me to calm before he greets me. Chloe does the same. He strokes us both under the chin a few times. "Good job, both of you," he says to us, and we wag our tails. Looking up, he says to the girls, "And both of you as well."

They beam back at him, and he introduces them to Rosa. He rests a hand on her arm, his eyes soft. I have to say I've never seen Miguel this mellow.

"Your music was wonderful," Rosa says to Tanya. "You have a such a beautiful voice."

Tanya flushes and thanks her. She glances over to her parents and brothers, standing in the line of people waiting to talk to the boss and Annie.

"Tell them congratulations for me," he says. "I'm not one for crowds."

Now that's the Miguel I know.

Molly smiles. "Dad will understand. And Annie definitely."

"I need to go get in line," Tanya says. She hands Chloe's leash to Miguel. "Annie told us to thank you again for keeping her."

Miguel shrugs. "Happy to do it. She's watched the kennel for me. And who knows?" He squeezes Rosa's hand and grins. "Maybe I'll ask her to return the favor."

Molly and Tanya exchange a wide-eyed look. And then Tanya says, "I'll save you a place," and cuts across the grass to join her family.

Miguel limps toward the parking lot, Rosa on one arm and holding Chloe's leash with his other.

"Wait!" Molly rushes after them. "I meant to ask, do you know Life Support Service Canines? They have a kennel in Manassas near you."

"I've heard of them," he says after a brief pause. "Haven't ever been there or met any of the people." Miguel smiles. "Or, more important, any of their dogs. Why?"

"A friend got a service dog from them, only it was a fake and hadn't been trained at all."

"Fake? They're selling fake dogs?" He frowns.

Molly flushes. "Sorry. I wasn't clear." She tells him about Jordan and how the people at Life Support had been spoofed. "They say they never saw Cooper—that's the dog. Annie doesn't think Cooper even knows how to detect low blood sugar."

Miguel's face goes still, the way it does when he's thinking. "Hard to believe they couldn't know anything about it," he says at last.

"That's what Jordan's mom thinks," Molly says. "But Dad says there are lots of fake websites these days." She pauses. "Anyway, just wondered if you knew them."

"I don't," he says slowly, as if he's still thinking. "But a friend of mine—another trainer—said something about them." He shakes his head. "Can't remember. I'll ask him and let you know."

With that, he and Rosa say goodbye and turn once more toward the parking lot. Molly and I head over and join Tanya and her family in line.

"Hey." Grady walks over to us. I stare at him. It's a good thing dogs have noses, because while this dressed-up guy with shiny shoes and slicked hair doesn't *look* like Grady, he still smells like him.

"You did great!" Grady says. "I don't know if I could get Snippet to be that good in church." He compliments Tanya on her singing. Then, moving closer, he says in a low voice to Molly, "I searched for Dyson Banks, but same story. No real hits. Must be another alias."

Molly frowns, but before she can say anything, Madison strolls up. "Aren't you two prettier than peach blossoms? And the singing was divine." She turns to Molly. "Honey why aren't you up in the reception line with your daddy?"

Molly's face colors and she shrugs. "Too awkward with Doodle," she says at last. "This way if he, um, needs anything I can take care of it."

What?

It takes a long time to get through the line. When we finally get up to the boss and Annie, they give Molly big hugs and for some reason all three of them get a little teary.

And then Mrs. Franklin, who has been waiting off to the side, asks, "You girls ready?"

We follow her out to her van. She doesn't have a crate in it, so I sit on the floor in front of Molly on the back seat.

Hey. We're going back to our new place.

"I can't believe Doodle is not invited to the reception," Mrs. Franklin says as she pulls into our driveway.

"The place doesn't allow dogs," Molly says.

Mrs. Franklin shakes her head, making a clicking sound. "If I were you, Doodle, I'd complain."

Hard to complain when no one understands you. Just part of the problem with communicating with humans.

Molly pulls a key from a tiny purse and opens the front door. "Ack!" she says as we go inside. "Hot in here."

I have to agree. Usually there's a little breeze coming in from the windows, but they're all shut tight. I start to pant before we're across the living room. Molly takes me through the back door, fending off Moxy who tries to run inside, and into the backyard. Fortunately, it's cooler here in the night air.

"It's just for a couple of hours," Molly says, "and Mom and I will be back to get you. Keep Moxy company!"

And then she goes back through the house, into Mrs. Franklin's van, and I hear it drive away.

After all the crowds and confusion of the wedding, it's nice to stretch out under the big tree in the dark and sink into the cool grass. Before long, Moxy comes cautiously across the lawn, and after a few tentative nose sniffs to make sure things are still good between us, curls up beside me. I nap to the contented purr of the kitten.

Sometime later, I hear a car pull into the driveway. Not the boss's or the Franklins' van, but one I've heard before. I jump up. Moxy, startled, tears across the yard and through the cat door. I run to the fence, barking, and stick my nose up to one of the skinny openings between the boards. A car door closes and I catch a scent. Definitely the same man as from the night before. I hear a clank and a lopping sound, and the gate suddenly swings open. A man stands on the other side, holding what look like giant pruners.

He calls to me. "Here, boy. Here!"

I stand back, not sure he's someone I want to go to. He comes toward me, and then pulls something from a grocery bag he's carrying. A piece of meat, by the smell of it. "Here boy. Here!"

Humans like to say that dogs don't have good memories, but there are certain things that dogs don't forget. When something goes spectacularly wrong, a dog remembers how it happened. And I remember that the last time a stranger held out a piece of food this way and I took it, things went spectacularly wrong. Not going to happen. I don't move.

"Here boy!"

I back away from him.

He curses, using words the boss never uses.

When I refuse to come closer, he runs deeper into the yard, trying to circle behind me.

It's no contest to keep away from him. My four legs give me much more speed than his two.

He angles around and then lunges at me. I easily leap away. He keeps coming at me and I run out through the gate and across the front yard. Try to catch me now!

But, instead of chasing me, he goes through the gate, jumps into his car and drives off.

What? No idea why he would do that. I sniff the driveway and gate area thoroughly burning the man's scent into my nose.

After that, I sit and study the neighborhood. A dog likes to know his surroundings, and except for a few walks, mainly to Cooper's and Tanya's houses, I haven't been out much in this new place. No better time to explore than now. I take off at a trot, turning into a few houses here and there to check out the scents.

I pass homes and apartment buildings, people sitting on their porches, some of them smoking. I pass people in their backyards barbecuing, and several dogs behind fences who bark death threats at me. A boy, younger than Molly, whizzes past me on a bike. I could keep up with him if I wanted, but it's warm, and I'm already panting.

I turn down the first side street, go a couple of blocks and turn again, making a broad circle which will eventually lead me back to the house. Some people in this area have trash cans out and I stop at a couple to smell what food remnants might be inside.

All in all, I'm having a fine time, but then I hear a voice. A loud voice, calling. I stop and listen.

"Doodle! Doooodle!"

Odd. The voice isn't Molly's or the boss's. It belongs to a boy. Not Grady, though.

"Doooodle!"

I head toward the sound and soon I see a figure with a flashlight walking down the road. "Doooodle," he calls. And then I recognize him. Jordan.

He must see me, too, because he says, "Doodle, come! Come here, boy. Come!"

I run up to him even though I hear tension in his voice which might normally make me cautious.

"Good boy! *Good* boy!" Now his voice is filled with relief. He grabs my collar, quickly attaching a leash. Not sure what's going on, but when he offers me a treat, I take it since Jordan isn't a stranger. Although a long drink of water is more what I could really use right now.

He whips out his phone. "I found him!" he says excitedly. "A block over from my street, just cruising down the road like he owned the place. We're heading toward my house."

And then, to my surprise, I hear Molly's voice on the other end. "Oh, that's wonderful. *Wonderful.* Oh, Jordan, this is so good! We're on our way."

But now I'm worried. Because Molly sounded really upset and I have no idea why.

Chapter 13

Unwelcome Surprises

"Doodle!" Molly exclaims, scooting out of Cori's car as soon as they've pulled up beside us. She's still in the dress she wore to the wedding. "Doodle, I was so worried!"

Her dress makes a crinkling sound as she runs over to me, throwing her arms around my neck, which is not something I normally like, except when it's Molly doing it. I lick her face, which I almost never do, but clearly she's distressed.

"Thanks so much," Molly says to Jordan, wiping her face and managing a half-laugh. "I can't thank you enough. I was so scared. The last time Doodle ran away . . ." Whoa. Her eyes water and she swallows.

I don't remember ever running away, but I do remember a time when Molly and I were separated for a long time and while that was an adventure, it wasn't a good one.

"I can't thank you enough," Molly says to Jordan. "I'm *so* glad I thought to call you. When we found the gate open . . ." She shakes her head.

Jordan smiles, looking genuinely happy. "Hey, you helped me find Cooper. We got to look out for each other, right? That's what neighbors are for."

"Right! Which reminds me—" Molly pulls out her phone, taps it and then says, "Tanya, we found him! Yeah. So you and your mom don't have to start searching. I'll call you back in a little bit and tell you everything."

"Tanya and her brothers were changing clothes and were going to help search," Molly explains, pocketing her phone. "I was so scared."

Jordan nods. "I know. I'm glad you called me."

Cori gets out of the car and walks over to us. She's no longer dressed like she was at the wedding but in her typical slacks and blouse.

Molly says, "Jordan, this is my mom, Ms. Vega. And this is Jordan Taylor."

Jordan gives her a nod, and Cori thanks him for finding me. To be clear, I *wasn't* lost. I was on my way home.

"You're the one who's a cop?" Jordan asks.

"A detective, yes," Cori says with a smile.

Jordan glances at Molly, who flushes and says, "I haven't asked her yet. It's been so busy."

"Ask me?" Cori raises her eyebrows.

Molly says, "Jordan and his mom got conned by this guy who sold them a fake service dog—one who wasn't well trained at all. And we were, um, wondering if you might have, um, contacts in Manassas who could investigate it."

Cori's mouth twists. "Ah," she says after short pause. "I might. But right now—" she gestures at me, for some reason "—it's late and we have a lot to do."

"Sure," Jordan says. "Just when you have time. Molly can tell you all about it."

After one more round of thanks, Molly switches Jordan's leash for my regular one and leads me to Cori's car. It's just a sedan, not a van, but even so the backseat is much roomier than the one in Annie's car. Cori drives back to our place.

For a moment, Cori and Molly stare at the open gate. Cori goes over to the fence and shines a flashlight on the gate and backyard. Then she gets on the phone.

"Like we thought when we first saw it," Cori says, as Molly and I come up beside her. "Chain's been cut. I called for an officer to come over and check it out. They'll be fifteen or twenty minutes. Oh, and there's a piece of meat on the grass. I guess Doodle didn't eat it."

"I'm glad he didn't," Molly exclaims. "Could be poison. *Good boy, Doodle!*"

We all go inside, and Molly runs to her room to change clothes.

"Hot in here," Cori says, looking around at the place. "But roomy."

"Yeah," Molly says from her room. "Dad got a couple of air conditioners but had trouble getting them up. It's a lot better when the windows are open."

Moxy starts to yowl from the mudroom.

"That the new kitten?" Cori tilts her head toward the sound.

"Yeah. She's an outdoor cat except for the mudroom."

"I wonder how long that will last," Cory asks, her voice dry.

Why does everyone keep saying that?

"Dad says forever." Molly comes out of her room wearing shorts and a blouse. "Our stuff is all right here," she says, waving a hand at the suitcase, kibble, and bags by the door. She and Cori load it all into the car, and then Molly comes back and grabs my leash and her camera, and we go back outside.

"They shouldn't be long," Cori says. "Don't touch anything."

"I know." Molly sounds a little offended. She starts taking photos. After a bit she stops. "Do you think I should call Dad? I would have had to if we hadn't found Doodle, but now . . ."

"But now there's not really anything he can do," Cori says firmly. "And it would ruin his honeymoon."

Molly nods. "That's what I was thinking." She's silent for a moment and then, staring into the yard, "Will they test that piece of meat? For poison?"

"I'll ask them to," her mother replies. "And test the gate for fingerprints. Whoever did this probably wore gloves, but it won't hurt to try."

And then I hear a siren and before long see flashing lights. A cop car pulls into our driveway and a short man with a moustache and a taller, stocky woman get out. Both are wearing uniforms. Cori shows them her ID and talks to them briefly.

"No sign that anyone entered the house?" the short cop asks Molly.

"No," she says, "just the backyard."

At some point, they pick up the piece of meat and put it into a bag. They spend a lot of time at the gate, too, smearing something on it. Molly watches it all with great interest.

Finally, the police are done. They say goodbye to Cori, and once again I get in the back of her car, which is more crowded now because Molly has one of her bags on the floor.

"I think I'd like a fingerprint kit," Molly says with some enthusiasm as we pull away.

"Mm." Cori keeps her eyes on the road. "It's no good without access to a database. And any prints you took wouldn't be admissible in court unless you could prove a clear line of evidence."

"Yeah." Molly sounds a little deflated. "Still, it'd be cool to know how to do it. Maybe you could teach me this week while I'm here."

"Mm. Maybe," Cori says without much commitment.

After that, they don't talk much and I nap because, frankly, it's been a really long day.

I wake up when the car slows to turn onto Cori's street. Lots of older, smaller houses in this neighborhood. Cori's is much the same as always, an older wood frame house with a bit of lawn and a strip of flowers by steps leading up to the front door. Not much yard here, front or back. The yards in this area aren't of a size that I'd call dog friendly.

Molly puts me on a leash, and we follow Cori to the door. I smell the flowers as well as Miga, Cori's cat, who is much bigger and fortunately much quieter than Moxy. Miga and I have been friends since the first time Molly and I visited.

Cori, carrying one of Molly's bags, unlocks the door and goes inside. The sound from a TV, volume high, blares from the house. We're just going through the open door when I hear Cori cry out in alarm.

"Benita!"

Benita slumps in her easy chair, eyes closed, one hand on her chest, the fingers of the other wrapped around a portable phone—the kind that are bigger than cell phones.

Cori leans over her, slapping her cheek lightly and speaking rapidly in Spanish.

Molly gasps and runs to her mother.

"She won't wake up," Cori says, her phone already in her hand.

"911," comes a voice through the receiver.

Cori rattles off her name and address and says, "I just came home and my aunt is unconscious. I think she might have had a heart attack or stroke. She's breathing, but her pulse is weak. She's 69 but has been in good health." She talks a little more and then pockets her phone.

"Ambulance will be here in a couple of minutes." She shakes her head, and strokes Benita's cheek. "*Despierta, tía,*" she whispers several times. And then to Molly, "She didn't come tonight because she said she was really tired. But other than that, she was okay when I came home to change after the wedding. She didn't seem sick or anything."

Molly, the color drained from her face, grabs a comforter from the back of the couch and hands it to her mother, who gently wraps it around Benita.

"I hope she'll be okay," Molly says in a small voice.

And then Cori whirls to face Molly and blurts, "What am I going to do with you?"

Molly stares at her.

Cori reaches out and touches her arm. "Sorry. I didn't mean it that way. But I'll need to be with her, and they won't allow you inside the hospital." She glances at me. "And certainly not Doodle. And I can't leave you here alone."

"We'd be okay," Molly says, without much enthusiasm. "I have Doodle to protect me."

Cori shakes her head vigorously. "I'd never forgive myself if something happened to you. And your dad would kill me."

"We could go with you and wait in the car," Molly suggests.

In the distance, I hear the faint sound of a siren.

Another shake of the head. "I'm not sure how safe that is either. We've had two calls out to Madison General in the last few weeks. That might be worse than leaving you here."

Molly frowns.

Cori goes still. "I hear the ambulance."

"Tanya!" Molly exclaims. "I could go to their place. Mrs. Franklin invited me before she knew I was coming here." She whips out her phone and presses keys.

"Hey, Tanya?" she asks in a strained voice. She explains the situation.

The siren suddenly goes silent, but lights flash from a vehicle pulling up to the curb.

Cori's at the door, gesturing to the EMTs, who rush into the house and over to Benita.

"We can stay at Tanya's," Molly announces. "Should they pick us up here or meet us at the hospital?"

It takes Cori a moment to answer. Her eyes are fixed on the EMTs.

"The hospital, I guess. In front of the emergency room. Madison General. Do they know where that is?"

Molly asks into her phone and then nods. "Mrs. Franklin has been there before. Tanya says they're leaving right now."

Cori nods and turns her attention back to her aunt.

Before long, the EMTs have loaded Benita onto a bed with wheels and are rolling it down the driveway.

Cori calls out to them, "I'll meet you there." She grabs Molly's suitcase. We hurry outside and bustle into the car, me in the back as usual.

Cori quickly backs out of the driveway and speeds after the ambulance, all her attention on the road.

But Molly huddles in the seat beside her, her face turned to the window, her thin shoulders moving as she silently cries.

Chapter 14

Home Away from Home

C ORI TURNS THE CAR INTO THE BRIGHTLY LIT HOSPItal parking lot, driving straight up to a covered drive-through leading to an even brighter entry with big glass doors, the kind that open and shut as you approach them.

"There they are!" Molly says, lowering her window and waving.

"Well, that's good," Cori's voice is tight and tense.

Molly scoots from the car and gets me out on the leash. Tanya bustles over, gives Molly a brief hug, and then takes one of her bags. Mrs. Franklin gets the others.

"Don't forget the trunk," Cori says. It pops open as she says that. Not sure how that happens. Molly takes me to the Franklins' van and returns to her mother's car for rest of the stuff, which includes my bag of kibble.

"Thanks!" Cori says, staring straight ahead. Without another word, she pulls out of the covered entryway and into the parking lot.

Tanya sits in the back seat beside Molly, me on the floor in front of them.

"Thanks for coming," Molly says. "Mom wouldn't let Doodle and me stay there alone and wait for her."

"And right she was!" Mrs. Franklin eases the van into the parking lot, and then out to the street. "She'd never forgive herself if something happened to you. And your daddy—he'd never forgive her!"

A ghost of a smile forms on Molly's face, the first in a long time. "Mom said almost those exact words."

"And you would be lonely and worrying and all by yourself," Tanya adds. "It'd be awful."

Molly nods, reaching down to touch my head. "I really didn't want to be alone."

Mrs. Franklin says, "It'd be terrible. What a day you've had! Enough going on for a month. The wedding, Doodle gone, an emergency . . ."

"Yeah." Molly's voice breaks. I lay my head on her knee.

"So what happened with Doodle?" Tanya asks. "You didn't have time to give me the whole story."

Molly clears her throat and then, in a stronger voice, explains how she and her mother arrived at our house to find the gate open. "Dad put a lock on the gate because of the trashcan incident, but it was chopped in two. And there was this piece of meat, like a small round steak or something, on the grass in the backyard. I think whoever broke in was trying to get Doodle to come to him."

"Good thing he didn't eat it!" Tanya exclaims.

"That's what I said. It could have been poison. Mom's going to get it tested." She reaches down and touches me under my chin. "You were too smart for that guy, weren't you?"

I have to agree. I'm always smart.

"Anyway, so I called you and Jordan, and then Mom and I drove real slow down the road with the windows open, calling Doodle."

"So scary!" Tanya breathes.

"Yeah. And did I tell you about Mrs. Dodds? How she said if she ever saw Doodle loose she'd call animal control?" Molly recounts the incident where she and Jordan passed the Dodds. "And we're pretty sure it's her son who's doing this. Mom called the local police after we got Doodle back and they came and took fingerprints.

"But first," Molly continues, "we drove up one street and down another and no sign of Doodle. And I was about to start calling the animal shelters. But then Jordan called. He found him about a block and a half on the other side of his home."

"Yikes," Tanya says. "That's far."

Not far if you're a dog. And, again, I knew perfectly well where I was.

"So we go get him, and then Mom has the cops come to the house and take fingerprints."

"And then you go to your Mama's and run straight into another emergency!" Mrs. Franklin makes a clicking sound.

"Yeah." Molly tells them how Cori found the TV on and Benita lying, eyes closed, in her easy chair. "Mom thought she was just asleep at first, but she couldn't get her to wake up. So she called the ambulance."

No one says anything for a moment. And then, sounding upset, Molly says, "Oh. I meant to ask Mom to text me when she knows how Aunt Benita is doing. I don't know if she'll remember."

"You can wait a while and then send her a text to remind her," Mrs. Franklin says.

Molly nods, but her face is unhappy. "I don't want to bother her if she's busy."

Molly often worries about bothering her mother, although not as much now as when they first started seeing each other again.

And then Mrs. Franklin pulls into the driveway, and everyone is busy bringing in Molly's and my stuff and getting Molly settled.

Did I mention this has been a long day? Frankly, I'm beat, and Molly and Tanya seem to be as well. So I'm glad when Molly says she's ready for bed and takes me out to pee in the Franklins' small backyard. I'm inspecting the perimeter, looking for the best spot, when I hear an alarming sound. Molly's crying.

I zoom back to her. She drops to one knee and puts her arms around my neck. "Oh Doodle," she says, her voice breaking. "Nothing will ever be the same again." I stand still, supporting her weight as her whole body shudders from the grief inside her. "And then you were gone," she says at one point in between sobs. "And I was so scared."

Light spills from the back door as it opens. Mrs. Franklin steps out. "Molly," she calls, "are you okay?"

Molly stands up. "Yeah," she says, but her voice breaks on the word.

Mrs. Franklin goes straight to her and opens her arms. Molly collapses into them, her shoulders moving as she cries.

"Oh, baby." Mrs. Franklin's voice is as soothing as a warm blanket. "Baby, it will be all right. I promise you, everything will be all right."

After a long time, Molly pulls away, straightens up and wipes her face on the inside of her blouse. "Sorry," she says in a small but steadier voice.

Mrs. Franklin pulls a tissue from her pants pocket and hands it to her. "Nothing to be sorry for. Change is hard. Even when it's good, it's hard. And then with everything else. . ."

Molly blows her nose.

"You know what I did the day we bought this house?" Mrs. Franklin asks.

Molly shakes her head.

"We were doing the final walk-through, and I shut myself in the bathroom so Lamar couldn't hear me and cried like a baby."

"Really?"

"Really. I was excited about the house—it was what we'd always wanted—but I was scared, too. So scared. The mortgage was the biggest payment we'd ever had in our lives. And I was worried some folks might not want a black family in the neighborhood. I'd had friends who'd had bad times in new places, you know? Our old apartment was small and crowded, but at least we knew everyone around us. Had friends. Felt part of the neighborhood. And here we were in a brand-new place and who knew how it'd turn out?"

Molly nods. "I know," she says in a thick voice.

"And you know what happened? That Lamar—sometimes I think the man is psychic! He knocked on the door. 'Barb,' he said, 'are you in there crying?'" She pauses and from her voice it sounds as if she's smiling. "And I opened that door and he took me in his arms and said, 'Whatever happens we have each other. And that's all that matters.'"

Mrs. Franklin pulls out another tissue and dabs her eyes. "It was like one of those Hallmark movies," she says shaking her head as if she still can't believe it, "and Lamar is usually the most unsentimental man on God's good earth. But he was right. And that move was the best thing we ever did—besides getting married and having our kids, that is."

Molly doesn't speak for a few moments. "And now we're closer to you," she says at last.

"And now you're closer to us. And can count on us whenever you need anything. And whatever happens, you will *always* have your dad. I know that for a fact. I know how much that man loves you."

Another silence. Then, in a stronger voice, Molly says, "Thanks."

She turns towards the door. I dash over to a bush to relieve myself and then catch up to her and Mrs. Franklin just as they go inside.

Tanya's waiting in the kitchen. She gives Molly a worried look but doesn't say anything. The girls get into their pajamas and brush their teeth. Molly starts to lie down on a pad on the floor by Tanya's bed, where she always sleeps when we stay over, but this time Tanya says, "You take the bed. You've had the worst day ever."

Molly gives her a grateful smile. "Okay. Thanks." She plugs in her phone, grabs her pillow—her favorite one that she takes everywhere—and stretches out on the bed. I lie down on the rug beside Tanya who reaches over to scratch my ears. "Kind of fun being down here with you, Doodle," she murmurs. And then I hear soft snores from both of the girls as I drift off to sleep.

Chapter 15

The Scene of the Crime

I WAKE UP THE NEXT MORNING WITH SUNLIGHT STREAM-ing in through thin curtains. The girls are still asleep. I get up, stretch, and pad out to the kitchen to find Mrs. Franklin putting pieces of bacon into a frying pan. Is this going to be a great day or what?

I've heard the boss say that he loves to get up to the smell of coffee, which is why he has this kind of coffee pot that will come on automatically in the morning. Coffee doesn't smell as bad as it tastes, thank heaven, but I still don't see the attraction. But I could wake up to the smell of bacon every morning of every day.

I lie in the doorway watching Mrs. Franklin fork strips of bacon into a frying pan. Honestly, bacon might possibly be the best scent in the world. While the bacon cooks, she whips some eggs in a bowl, adds a little milk and salt and pepper and fries those up in a separate pan. Then she pulls a bowl from the fridge, gets out a griddle, and spoons batter onto it. Pancakes!

We don't usually do big breakfasts at our house. The boss and Molly are more cereal and milk types, and of course I'm stuck with kibble. If I'm lucky, Molly will pour a little of her left-over milk into my bowl when she's done.

You can see why I love to come here. Not only is the food great, I know Mrs. Franklin will save a little of everything for me.

Pretty soon Mr. Franklin comes out and sits down. He's already wearing his mechanic's uniform for work. The boss calls him a wizard under the hood, a baffling description, to be sure. I think it means he's very good at fixing cars, which is what he does for a living.

Derrin and Tyson come next and start setting the table at Mrs. Franklin's request. And then Kenny, rubbing his eyes, stumbles over to a chair.

"I don't know whether to call the girls or let them sleep." Mrs. Franklin sets a plate of pancakes on the table, next to the platter of bacon and the scrambled eggs.

"Let them sleep," Mr. Franklin says.

With bacon on the table? Bad choice in my opinion.

Mrs. Franklin sinks into a chair beside her husband and bows her head along with everyone else while Mr. Franklin says a short prayer.

And then they all heap food on their plates and start to eat.

I hear sounds in the bathroom, and then Molly comes out. "Bacon!" she breathes. "And pancakes!" She has dark circles under her eyes and still looks worn out, but she gives Mrs. Franklin a big smile and sits down to fill her plate.

Tanya joins us soon after.

"Any news from your mother?" Mrs. Franklin asks.

Molly, her mouth full, shakes her head. After she swallows, she says, "I checked my phone when I first got up. Nothing."

"What about your dad? Does he know you're here now?"

"I was thinking about texting him. But . . ." she frowns. "He's on his honeymoon. And they're hiking in the mountains and he might not even have phone reception."

"So he doesn't know about Doodle?" Mrs. Franklin asks.

Molly shakes her head again. "Didn't want to ruin the honeymoon. And Mom said there was nothing he could do. If we hadn't found Doodle, it would have been different."

Everyone seems to agree.

"It was a beautiful wedding," Mrs. Franklin says, and there are nods around the table.

"And Tanya was great on her solo!" Molly adds.

There's more conversation, but somehow I doze off until I hear the clank of silverware on plates. I'm instantly awake. I sit up, keeping my eyes fixed on Mrs. Franklin.

"I think someone's ready for his breakfast," Mrs. Franklin says, noticing my stare.

Molly scoops some kibble into my dish. Not my meaning at all. But Mrs. Franklin stirs in a tiny amount of bacon grease as well as bits of eggs scraped from the plates along with several large bites of pancakes soaked in syrup. And, with a glance around as if she's doing something sneaky, she tops it off with a whole piece of crumbled bacon. Delicious!

It turns out to be Tyson and Tanya's day to clean up after breakfast, so of course Molly helps, too. Then she takes me out to do what the boss calls "my business" and scoops it up afterward. The yard is nowhere near as big as ours, but it makes up for it by being somewhere different. Dogs like to have variety in where they pee and poop.

"Do you think we could go feed Moxy?" Molly asks after we come back in.

"Good idea!" Tanya says. They put the question to Mrs. Franklin.

"I don't know, given what's gone on there. Maybe I should go with you."

The girls don't look too enthusiastic about the idea.

"But it's broad daylight. Nothing ever happened at our place except at night," Molly says. "Plus, we'll have Doodle."

The girls wait in silence as Mrs. Franklin considers it, her hand on her broad hips. "I guess. But keep your eye out for anything unusual." She fixes them both with a stern look. "And if you see something, leave the crime fighting to the police. Understood?"

"Yes, ma'am," Tanya says.

Molly adds, "We will. Promise."

Molly puts on my walking collar and we take off.

I've never walked to our new place from Tanya's. It's not very far at all, only a block and a half. It's a fine day, cooler than it's been, with a stiff breeze crammed with all sorts of scents.

The gate is still open, as it was when we left last night. With a glance in every direction that reminds me of Mrs. Franklin with the bacon, Molly turns the door key into the lock and goes inside.

"Whew! Hot!" Tanya exclaims.

"Yeah. Maybe we should open a few windows while we're here." They go through the house, opening windows and leaving the front door open with the screen door locked. Then, we all go toward the yowling in the mudroom to see Moxy.

Tanya picks her up, while Molly fills her food and water dish, scoops out the litter—which I could take care of if only they'd let me—and checks the cat door. Then we all go into the backyard. Molly shows Tanya where the lock was cut. "You can see the powder where they took the fingerprints," she says. "But Mom says that it won't do any good unless the prints are already in the system. And I bet the Dodds' fingerprints aren't. Dad says her son looks like a loser, but he didn't look like a criminal."

"What do criminals look like?" Tanya has a surprising edge to her voice.

Molly gives her a puzzled look.

"It's just that Derrin's always saying people look at him suspiciously because he's tall and black, and there was that drug thing with Kenny where everyone thought he was bad because he was black. And they're straight A students."

Molly doesn't answer for a second. "I didn't mean black," she says earnestly. "I guess I meant scruffy and wearing an old hoody and reeking of beer. But you're right. The biggest crooks we've found looked like average people, just like Kenny and Derrin or Grady or Dad."

Tanya nods, and leans in to inspect the gate. "Here's a place without powder. Maybe they missed a section. I wonder if anyone can buy a fingerprint kit. I bet they sell them online."

Molly perks up at this. "Great idea! I have some money saved up."

"And then maybe we could somehow get the fingerprints of the Dodds and compare them."

Molly says, "Oh, that'd be great." She thinks for a moment. "I know what their car looks like. I bet we could get fingerprints from there."

She and Tanya stare at each other for a second and then do a high five. We go back inside, leaving Moxy in the mudroom. She immediately starts meowing in her loud, obnoxious voice.

The girls quickly shut up all the windows, and Molly carefully locks the front door.

A glint catches my eye. Something shiny in the bushes by the porch steps. I go toward it as far as the leash will allow, working my nose.

Molly says, "Doodle, don't pull." But then she says, "What is it?"

I lead her down the steps and as I get closer, catch a familiar scent. Beer. And then I see it, slightly crumpled and partially hidden under a bush.

"A beer can!" Molly bends over and peers at it. "Not ours, that's for sure."

"Don't touch it," Tanya warns. "If we get the fingerprint kit, we can take prints."

"Yeah. I bet the cops missed this."

The girls talk about this in excited voices all the way back to the Franklins'.

I can still smell the bacon when we go inside. The girls hurry to Tanya's room and huddle around Tanya's laptop.

"Here's one for only $10," Tanya says. "And another for $30."

"I wonder how accurate the $10 one would be? And how long it'd take to get here?" Molly studies the screen. "But I'd have to call Dad to see if he'd let me order it on his card."

"You need to call him anyway."

"Yeah, but if he asks why I want a fingerprint kit . . ." Molly frowns.

"You've said before you want to be a detective like your mom," Tanya says.

"But maybe Mom has an extra one I could have," Molly answers. "And save my camera money."

They talk like this for some time while I take a little nap on the floor beside them. I wake up when Molly's phone chimes.

She looks at the screen. "It's Mom," she says to Tanya. "I'll put it on speaker." She taps the phone. "Hey, Mom. How's Aunt Benita?"

"Okay." Cori sounds exhausted. "It was a stroke. She's going to be okay, probably, but they're going to keep her a week or so. Sometimes after a stroke like this there's a danger of a second or third one."

"Like earthquake aftershocks?"

A pause. "Maybe. I guess. But I'm going to be spending all my time off work at the hospital for a while. Are you doing okay at the Franklins? I think it might be better if you stayed there."

"Yeah," Molly says, not looking as disappointed as she often does when her mother cancels something. Which, I have to say, is kind of often. "We're doing great, and we can walk over to take care of Moxy."

"Don't go to that house alone," Cori sounds suddenly worried.

"I won't. Tanya and Doodle go with me, and we're only there for a few minutes."

"Good," her mother says. "It's not the time for any heroic crime fighting." Somehow, she sounds just like Mrs. Franklin. Another pause. "Anyway, I'm sorry about this week. I was really looking forward to it."

Now Molly's face turns sad. "Me too," she says in a small voice. But then, rallying, "But taking care of Aunt Benita is way more important."

"I was thinking that maybe, if she's doing better, I can pick you up during visiting hours and you can see her. I know that would cheer her up a lot."

"That'd be great," Molly says, brightening. "Anytime."

They talk a few minutes more before Cori says goodbye.

"I didn't ask about the fingerprint kit," Molly says.

Tanya nods. "Not after the 'don't do anything heroic' speech."

They both laugh.

"So I guess I need to call Dad. Or try to. Who knows if he has reception or not?" She stares at her phone, not moving. Finally, she sighs and presses a key. "Here goes nothing."

But the boss answers right away. "Molly!" he says, his voice happy and welcoming. "How's it going?"

"Good . . . but I'm at Tanya's." She tells the boss about finding Benita, and her mother having to stay with her at the hospital."

"Oh, I'm sorry. Is there . . ." he hesitates, "a prognosis?"

"Mom said she should be okay but might need some rehab."

"Oh, good. I like Benita. I'm glad it's not worse. Everything else okay?" the boss asks.

Molly bites her lower lip and glances at Tanya. "Yeah, fine. Moxy is lonely, but she's fine. We opened the windows and aired out the house while we were there." She takes a deep breath. "But you know how I might want to go into forensics someday? There's this fingerprint kit on Amazon for $30. Can I get it and pay you back with the money I've saved? Tanya and I thought it would be fun to practice while I'm here."

The boss doesn't answer right away. "I guess that'd be okay. You know my login, right?"

"Yeah." She recites something to him that makes no sense to me.

"That's it," he says cheerfully. And then, more seriously, "Don't use it to get anything else."

"I won't," Molly promises. "How's the honeymoon?"

"Wonderful!" the boss says, with such enthusiasm that Molly blushes.

"Okay, well, I just wanted to let you know I'm here and not at Mom's."

They say goodbye. Tanya flashes a thumbs up sign when Molly closes her phone. "I've got it up on my laptop still."

Molly goes over and types some stuff on the keyboard. "For four dollars more, we could get it tomorrow."

"I'll pay for that," Tanya says. "This is going to be fun."

"Nothing heroic," Molly murmurs, typing. When she's done, Tanya says, "So you didn't tell him about Doodle."

Molly sighs. "He sounded so happy. If I told him, he'd get all worried. I know he would. And he might guess why we wanted the fingerprint kit and say no." Molly's hand reaches up to twist a strand of hair. "I hope he's not mad when he finds out."

"There's nothing he can do, and Doodle is safe."

"Yeah," she says. "I just hope he sees it that way."

Chapter 16

True Detectives

TODAY, AFTER BREAKFAST, WHICH ALAS DOES NOT include bacon, Molly, Tanya, and I go over to the new house to check on Moxy. The gate still's open. Molly checks out the beer can, still in the same place, and takes some photos of it. Then we all go inside the house, which is hot, and the girls quickly put food out for Moxy and scoop out the litter box.

"We'll be back later," Molly promises the yowling kitten, who sounds very unhappy to have us leave. "As soon as we get the fingerprint kit."

We start walking, but Molly suddenly stops, frowning at the horizon. "Do you think we should get the can now? There's a chance of rain today, and it could wash off any fingerprints that might be on it."

"Good idea," Tanya says and so we turn around. Molly unlocks the house again and slips inside, coming back a few minutes later with a rubber glove and a plastic bag. She uses the glove to pick up the can, holding it by one edge as she drops it into the bag that Tanya holds open. And then, Molly takes the glove back inside, locks up again, and we head back to the Franklins'.

And wait for the box. At least the girls wait. I take a nap. It doesn't come before lunch, which turns out to be peanut butter sandwiches that the girls make for themselves because Mrs. Franklin is at work. Just before giving me her crust, Molly says, "I hope we didn't waste that four dollars."

But then I hear the sound of the UPS van—can't miss that—and the girls do, too. "It's here!" Tanya cries. They run to the door and bring in a box, which they quickly open.

Tyson, who's playing a video game in the living room, stops it and gets up. "What's that?"

When the girls tell him and why they want a fingerprint kit, he says, "Cool!" and hangs around watching while they get everything out.

Tanya reads the instructions out loud. Then she gets a couple of old newspapers from a box by the kitchen door and spreads them on the table. "Mama would kill us if we got this table stained with black powder." Soon, she takes Molly's and Tyson's prints, Molly takes hers and, after calling Kenny upstairs, his prints.

"I think we know how to do it," Tanya says, after washing the ink off her fingers.

"Now for the rest of the evidence," Molly says, agreeing. She and Tanya exchange a look.

Tanya tells Kenny that we're going to take fingerprints at Molly's place. "We won't be long," she promises.

"Okay," he says, heading down to the basement. "Don't get into trouble!"

Tyson goes back to his video game in the living room.

Tanya puts some of the fingerprint stuff in a bag and slings it over her shoulder. Molly grabs her camera and gets my walking collar and leash. "Doodle, want to go for a walk?"

Do dogs like treats? Of *course* I want to go for a walk. Although once we get outside, I'm surprised by how hot it is. The kind of heat where the air pushes down on you, heavy, full of water. I'm panting by the time we've reached the sidewalk.

"Hot!" Tanya fans her face with her hand as we walk.

Molly says, "It's good Kenny's babysitting. He doesn't ask as many questions as your mom."

Tanya laughs. "Don't tell Mama," she says. "We *love* it when Kenny's in charge."

We walk past our place and past Jordan's and turn down a road. Hey, I recognize this street. We're coming down it in the opposite direction, but this is the road where we met the Dodds the other day.

"That's it," Molly says, pointing at a flat-topped two-story brick building. She frowns. "But I don't see their car. It was parked in front when we were here the other day."

Tanya wipes the sweat from her forehead. "I bet they have parking in back." She points to a gravel lane that leads to the back of the building.

I suddenly feel Molly's tension coming down the leash. "Do you think it's legal?" she asks. "To go back there?"

They both stop walking, staring at the place. "I don't know," Tanya says. "If someone stops us, we could say we're looking for a friend or something."

Molly smiles. "You'd make a good detective. Or crook."

Tanya laughs, and we head down the lane. At the back, there is a gravel parking area with several cars.

"Not here," Molly says, her voice a mixture of relief and disappointment. "We'll have to try later." She glances at the sky which is considerably darker now than when we left. "If it doesn't rain."

She turns and we all walk briskly back to the sidewalk.

"Your place then," Tanya says, wiping her face again. "Before the fingerprints melt."

But we've only taken a few steps when Molly stops dead. "There! Across the street!" She points to a line of cars parked in front of several homes.

She leads us to an older sedan snug against the curb, nestled between a pickup and an SUV. With a furtive glance in every direction, Molly goes to the passenger side.

Tanya pulls a brush and the can of powder from her bag. "You keep watch," she says, "while I do this handle. And you can do the other one."

Molly nods. I don't know what she's watching for, but I stay on alert in case she's expecting trouble. So far, the street is quiet except for the sound of a mower somewhere near the end of the block.

Ducking down, Tanya quickly spreads the black powder on the handle, and then lifts the powder off with pieces of tape that she deposits into a little baggie.

A boom of thunder makes Molly jump. She's as nervous as a cat in a crate with a rottweiler, but I don't know why. She's not usually afraid of thunderstorms and there's still no traffic on the street. A breeze comes up and the air is suddenly much cooler.

Tanya gets up and shoves the bag into Molly's hand, taking my leash. "I think I got some good ones."

Molly goes through the same procedure with the powder and tape on the driver's side door handle.

As she stands up, another huge clap of thunder shakes the air around us.

"Let's get out of here," Molly says, giving Tanya the bag and grabbing my leash. We all take off at a run, just as lightning strikes close by, followed by a huge boom. Fat drops of rain pelt down on us. By the time we get to Tanya's house, my head and paws are wet, and the girls' feet and hair are soaked.

We all dash through the door, the girls giggling as they stand dripping on the floor.

"Tyler, get us some towels!" Tanya shouts.

Tyler angles his long body off the couch and stares at us like we're crazy. But then he runs into the bathroom and comes back and tosses each girl a towel.

"Did you get any?" he asks.

"Think so," Tanya huffs, rubbing the towel over her hair. "We won't know for sure until we check."

Molly wipes herself down, and then does my head, back, and paws. She and Tanya mop up the drops of water on the floor and then go into Tanya's room, returning shortly in dry clothes.

I have a long drink from the water bowl Mrs. Franklin keeps for me by the kitchen door, while the girls get glasses of lemonade. Then I stretch out on the cool wooden floor. Tanya spreads more newspaper on the table and soon she is bent over studying the pieces of tape.

Molly brushes the powder on the beer can she collected earlier, places pieces of tape on the powder and carefully lifts them off. Then, just as carefully, she presses the pieces of tape onto cards.

"Good one!" she says at one point. "This can be our base print. Hope it's not from some random litterer passing by."

"Amen!" Tanya says with fervor. She picks up something that looks like a small mirror with a handle, but is clear glass. I go over to sniff it.

"Look, Doodle," she says. "It makes things look bigger." She holds the glass up to the card and the fingerprint does seem larger, but smells the same, so I don't get what she's doing.

She and Molly take turns holding it up and studying all the cards, at first with eagerness, but growing glummer as they continue.

"No matches," Molly says at last, sounding discouraged. "I could have sworn we'd find one."

"Yeah. Maybe the beer can was from some random jerk after all."

"It'd be a coincidence. We've never had anyone do that before."

"In what? The two weeks you've been there?" Tanya asks. "I mean, it's a small data sample, like Ms. Mandisa was always talking about. Small samples can give misleading results."

"Yeah. Well we got zero results."

"We could go back and try the gate. See if there's anything left after the rain."

"Or by the police who already took prints." Molly sighs. "I'd call and ask my Mom if she's heard back on those, but with Benita . . ."

"I know." Tanya glances up to the clock on the wall. "But Mama's going to be home soon so we'd better clean this up."

Out of the window, lightning flashes with a boom so strong that the walls vibrate. The lights flicker.

"Wow!" Tanya says. "Another storm. I hope we don't lose power."

They get busy putting away the stuff on the table. Outside, there is more thunder and lightning, and then the sound of heavy rain. By the time I hear Mrs. Franklin's van pull into the driveway, the table is as bare and clean as always, and the thunder less frequent and farther away.

"There's Mama," Tanya says.

Tyson leaps up, clicks off the TV, grabs his game stuff and disappears downstairs.

Mrs. Franklin comes in, shaking the rain off her clothes. She sinks down into her favorite chair with a little sigh.

"What you girls been up to?" she asks, her head against the back of the chair and her eyes closed.

Tanya and Molly exchange a look. Then, Molly says, "Fingerprinting!" She explains about ordering the fingerprint kit. "When I watched the cop take fingerprints of our gate, I thought it'd be cool to learn to how to do it." She pauses. "Dad said it was okay to buy it. And it came today. We practiced on Kenny and Tyson and ourselves, so we'd know how to do it."

"And then Doodle found a beer can at Molly's place when we fed Moxy that we think the cops missed," Tanya adds. "And we brought it home and got a perfect print."

Mrs. Franklin's eyes pop open. "And what you gonna do with that?" she asks, suddenly alert.

Another shared glance between the girls.

"Maybe see if my mom will run it through her database to see if anyone comes up," Molly says. Mrs. Franklin nods, looking relieved. "That's a good idea. Sure like to get whoever's low enough to let a dog out in the street."

Neither of them mentions our walk to the Dodds or the car.

Molly's phone chimes. She glances at the screen, looking surprised. "Hey Jordan."

"Cooper's gone!" Jordan's voice is stringy with tension.

"What?"

Molly taps her phone and suddenly Jordan's words come through much louder. Mrs. Franklin and Tanya both listen intently.

"We were walking and he started getting nervous every time we'd hear thunder, so I decided we'd better go back home, but then there was this huge bang of thunder and he just ripped the leash from my hand and ran off." The words tumble from him as if he can't get them out fast enough. "So I ran after him and called him, but he just disappeared down the street. And Mama's at work so I don't have a car."

His breath catches and he sounds like him might be crying. "Plus she's going to kill me when she finds out because I'm not supposed to walk Cooper while she's gone, even though I'm almost thirteen and not a little kid." This last sounds bitter.

"We'll help you search," Molly assures him. "Where are you now. At home?"

"No. I'm . . . on the corner of . . ." Jordan pauses a second then rattles off some names.

Tanya gives her mother a questioning look.

From her chair, Mrs. Franklin shuts her eyes briefly, sighs deeply, and then heaves herself up. "Dogs are going to be the death of me," she says.

No idea what she means. Mrs. Franklin loves dogs.

"Tell him I'll go and pick him up and we'll search by car while you kids search on foot. Call Tyson and Kenny to help."

"I can grab extra leashes from our place," Molly says. "Did you hear that?" she asks Jordan.

"Yeah. Thanks. Thanks so much. I didn't know what to do."

"Ask him if he has his insulin with him," Mrs. Franklin says, "just in case."

"Not insulin," Jordan says, obviously hearing her. "It has to be refrigerated. But I have these tubes of glucose that I can squirt down my throat—or someone else could. Mama made me promise to always keep some on me."

"Good. Wait there. I won't be long." Mrs. Franklin goes into the kitchen and comes back with an umbrella.

Molly says goodbye and closes her phone.

We troop out to the van. Mrs. Franklin drives Tanya, Molly, and me to our new house where Molly grabs some extra leashes.

"I ought to get some of those to keep on hand if I'm going to be searching for dogs every other day," Mrs. Franklin grumbles. "I'm going to drop this leash off for Kenny and Tyson and then pick up Jordan."

Tanya and I take off, calling for Cooper as we go. The sidewalks and streets are wet, but the rain has stopped although the trees still drip down on us when we're under them.

We search for a long time. Molly and Tanya send lots of texts, and by the beeping on their phones receive them as well. But by the looks on their faces, the texts are never good news.

Finally, as it starts to get dark, we have to quit searching.

When Mrs. Franklin comes to pick us up, Jordan is slumped on the seat beside her, looking damp and miserable.

"Thanks for trying," he says to Molly and Tanya. He sounds near tears.

"We won't give up. I'll call all the shelters tomorrow," Molly says. "He has to be somewhere. He can't just disappear."

"Stupid dog," Jordan says, his voice at once angry and sad. "Stupid, stupid dog." He swipes a hand across his eyes. "And stupid me for taking him out."

After that, he says nothing, and when Mrs. Franklin drops him off, he walks head down to the door, and disappears inside.

"That dog," Mrs. Franklin says. "Going to be the death of me."

"Or of Jordan," Tanya says, and Molly and Mrs. Franklin nod in agreement.

Chapter 17

Rehab

The first thing Molly and Tanya do after breakfast—which is only oatmeal—is to start calling animal shelters. Molly finds the numbers on the computer and then Tanya calls them.

"Discouraging," Tanya says after several calls. "Where could he be?"

"Maybe someone found him and is keeping him," Molly says. "He's a good-looking dog. Annie says it happens all the time, that people find a stray and just keep it rather than try to find the owner."

"That's selfish," Tanya says with indignation. "They should know people are looking. I mean, with Moxy, we asked around and you put up signs, right?"

Molly nods.

"So if someone wanted her back, they'd know where she was." Tanya shakes her head. "Poor Jordan. He was so excited to have that dog."

"I know," Molly says. "Which is why we have to find this Kirby Banes or Dyson Banks or whoever he is."

Molly's phone chimes. "Maybe it's a shelter," she says, suddenly hopeful. Then, blinking in surprise, she puts her phone to her ear. "Hi, Mom."

Normally I can hear the person on the other end of the phone, but Tanya has music playing from her computer and it's too loud.

Molly's face brightens and she says, "Oh, good." She listens some more and says, "Sure. That'd be great!" And then, "Really? Yeah. We can do that!"

When she closes her phone, she says, "Mom is going to come by and pick us up to go see Benita at the rehab center. She has the day off."

"Us?" Tanya asks.

"Doodle and me," Molly says with excitement. "She said since Doodle's a Canine Good Citizen he's allowed in hospitals." Molly frowns a little. "I think she's mixing up the CGC and the AKC Therapy Dog Program, which is the one that can help dogs get into places like hospitals. Doodle hasn't done that yet. You have to do the CGC first."

"But Doodle will be good anyway, right? He goes everywhere with your dad."

Molly nods. "Yeah. He'll be fine. And it'll be fun to take him." She jumps up. "I've got to get ready."

Molly only changes clothes twice before settling on a lightweight blouse and pair of pants and sandals.

"I like those capris," Tanya says, which seems to make Molly happy. And then Tanya's eyes widen. "Your mom!"

Molly gives her a quizzical glance.

"The fingerprints!"

"Oh, yeah. How could I forget?" Molly gets her backpack, and she and Tanya carefully insert the baggy with the can and the bags holding the prints. Then Molly takes my plain harness, not the bed bug one, and puts it on me.

By the time we step outside into the warm, muggy morning, Cori is turning into the driveway.

She drives us back to the hospital where she took Benita the night of the wedding, but pulls into a different entrance, one around in the back.

Molly, plainly excited, says, "I can't believe you talked them into it!" We walk through a set of doors that spread open when we approach. Always been somewhat of a mystery to me, doors that do that. And a little unnerving, to be honest.

"This is so fun. I've always thought Doodle would make a great therapy dog."

Cori smiles down at her daughter. "It didn't take much talking really. They have a group of established therapy dogs who come in several times a week to visit the rehab patients. I told them Doodle had his certificate from the AKC, right? The one that says he a good citizen and can do this therapy work?"

Molly hesitates just a fraction before saying, "Yeah. The CGC."

"And I said he also works as a bed bug dog and is used to being in all sorts of public places." Cori chuckles. "They told me he could visit as long as he didn't find any bed bugs."

Molly laughs, although I'm not sure why. I only find bugs when they're there. I'd think they'd want to know if they were. But, weirdly enough, as I've mentioned before, sometimes people don't want to know.

All hospitals smell about the same, in my admittedly limited experience. Disinfectant, lingering faint food smells, spiced with the variety of odors people bring in on their shoes and their bodies.

A woman behind a desk just inside the door leans over and smiles down at me. "Therapy dog?" she asks.

Molly nods, waving at the CGC patch on my vest which she just sewed on this morning.

The woman gives us both a big smile. "I think the dogs help patients almost more than anything." She puts a finger to her lips and winks. "But don't tell the doctors."

We walk down a long shiny floor, my nails clicking on the surface, past a bunch of closed doors with signs on them Never been wild about these kinds of floors. Too slippery.

"They moved her here last night right after dinner," Cori says. "She's really doing well except she's not quite stable when walking and she's still slurring some of her words. But really, she's much better. For the first couple of days, she could hardly speak at all, and it was always in Spanish. I worried she might have lost all her English. And she can chew and swallow. If she couldn't do that, it'd be much worse."

Molly says, "Scary."

"It was." Cori sighs and her face shows her exhaustion. "But we're over the hump now. And we're lucky. It could have been much worse."

We turn down a hall and walk in a different direction. This hall has lots of open doors, though, and as we pass, we can see people in beds, some sitting up, some lying down, some with visitors. It would be easy to get lost in this place.

"Good thing you know where you're going," Molly says, echoing my thoughts.

Cori grins. "It's a maze, all right." She raises a hand. "Over there. 206."

As soon as we enter the room, my nose detects a familiar scent—Benita! She's in one of those beds that can go up or down, this one about halfway up. Her eyes are closed and the lines in her face cut deeper than I remember seeing before.

Molly stares at her a second, her eyes wide and dismayed, her face going pale.

"Benita," Cori says softly, "I have someone to see you."

Benita's eyes flutter open, and then recognition floods her face. "María!"

María is Molly's middle name and Benita always calls her that. She told her once she learned to call her María when Molly was little—before her mother left—and is too old to change her ways. And Molly doesn't seem to mind.

"Aunt Benita!" Molly goes over to the bed and takes the old woman's hand. "How are you doing?"

Benita answers, her words slow and a little hard to understand, but her eyes alert. "Better. Want. To. Go. Home."

"You will," Cori says reassuringly. "Two weeks, I think, if we can get you moving and speaking a little better."

"You scared us," Molly says, still holding Benita's hand.

"Scared. Myself," Benita admits. And then she seems to notice me for the first time. "Doool."

Molly leads me forward and Benita rests a hand on my head for a moment. She smiles at me. "Good. Dog."

After a bit, I get tired and lie down on the shiny floor. Here, the smell of disinfectant is much stronger. Cori sits in a chair by the bed and Molly stands, bending over her aunt while they talk about Benita's stroke, Molly and me going to the Franklins', and other things. Benita takes a long time to respond to questions. I drift off.

A nurse comes in after a while, waking me up. She's carrying a food tray. Molly and I scoot out of her way and she sets the food in front of Benita.

There something about hospital food that always smells a little old, a little stale.

Benita might think so, too, because she grimaces at Cori.

While Benita eats, Molly tells her about the wedding.

"Sorry. To. Miss. It." Benita says, laying down her fork for a bit.

It takes Benita a long time to eat, as her hand with the fork takes forever to get from her plate to her mouth. It seems everything about Benita has slowed down, like those football scenes the boss watches where the players move very slowly. When at last she finishes, she leans her head back and closes her eyes. Molly lifts the tray and places it on the small table by the bed.

Not long after, another nurse comes in. This one is a muscular Latino, with strong dark arms and a big smile.

"Ready for today's workout?" he asks Benita.

She sighs. "I. Guess. I. Have. To."

"You bettcha. It's your ticket out of this place. *Comprende?*"

"*Sí, señor*," she answers with a smile.

He gives Cori and Molly a friendly nod but stops dead when he sees me.

"Well, look at you!" he says. "I bet you're making everyone feel better today." He reaches down and places his large hand on my head. Then, turning to Cori, he says, "Is he a standard poodle? Don't see many of those here. Mostly Labradors and Goldens."

"He's my daughter's dog," Cori says, with a bend of her head toward Molly.

Molly beams at him. "A labradoodle, but he takes after the poodle side."

"Well, he's a handsome dude. I bet he's a hit with all the patients."

"We've only been here with Benita," Molly says. "He's not an official therapy dog." Then, adding quickly, "but we got permission."

"No problem. As long as he behaves, he's welcome. I'm going to take Miss Benita here to do a little therapy. Feel free to take him into the rooms with open doors on your way out. I'm sure the patients would love it."

Molly flushes and says, "That would be fun."

She and Cori give Benita a quick hug. "It was great seeing you," Molly tells her before we head out to the hall. Cori surges ahead, setting a brisk pace, with Molly and me following behind her.

As we come past a room with an open door, Molly hesitates, glancing wistfully inside, but Cori doesn't notice. Molly sighs and hurries to catch up to her mother.

An orderly pushing a gurney with an incredibly old, very pale woman on it passes us going the opposite direction. Behind the gurney, a woman using a walker limps slowly toward us.

As we come up to the woman, she raises her head. "Molly Hunter and Doodle! What are you doing here?"

Hey. I recognize her. How'd I miss her scent?

Molly's face lights up. "Mrs. Thomas! We're here to visit my aunt. She had a stroke a few days ago." And then, her eyes on the walker, she asks, "Are you . . . are you *here*?"

"'Fraid so," Mrs. Thomas says. "You'd think walking every day, sore knees or not, and trying to eat right would protect you from a stroke, but not always so. I had one four days ago."

"Oh." Molly's eyes are dark with sympathy. "I'm so sorry."

"Could be worse. I could be dead." Mrs. Thomas gives her a crooked grin. "I'm going to be okay. Just got to get this bum right leg working properly. But at least my brain's okay. Well, okay as it's ever been." She winks at us. "Leafy greens and blueberries."

Lost me there.

"What about you?" Mrs. Thomas asks, looking suddenly concerned. "Why are you here?"

"My aunt," Molly answers. "Well, my mom's aunt, really. She had a stroke on the night of my Dad's wedding." Molly glances up at Cori, who has turned and come back to us. "Mom, this is Mrs. Thomas. She owns the house we're renting."

"Oh, nice place! They're lucky to have it!" Cori says with enthusiasm. "Cori Vega. I'm Molly's mom."

"Yeah, we really love the house," Molly adds.

Mrs. Thomas smiles. "I'm glad you're enjoying it." She turns to Cori. "How long is your aunt in for?"

Cori laughs. "You make it sound like a prison sentence."

"There *are* similarities," Mrs. Thomas says in a dry voice.

Cori laughs. "We don't know yet. She's still pretty weak and has a fair amount of rehab to do. What about you?"

"Probably another week. They want me to be able to walk without fear of falling." She turns to Molly. "If you come back to see your aunt, drop by my room to say hello. Gets lonely here."

Molly says with enthusiasm, "We will!" And then, after a round of goodbyes, we continue down the long hall with the shiny floor.

After several turns and a fair amount of time, we reach the exit door. Can't say I'm sorry. Not at all fond of the smells in this place. And it's good to have decent footing again.

When we get back to the car, Molly opens the back door. While I hop in, she picks up the backpack she brought, unzips it, and moves it to the front seat.

"Mom, guess what? I need your help." She says this in a bright voice, but there's a note of strain beneath the cheerful tones.

Cori eases the car out of the parking lot. "For what?" she asks, sounding suddenly cautious.

"You know how I said I'd like to learn how to do fingerprints?"

A slight pause. "Yes?"

"Well." Molly takes a deep breath, and then the words come quickly. "There are lots of kits you can buy online and Dad said I could buy one, so I did with my own money. And we practiced taking prints and checking them—Tanya and me—and then we found this beer can at our new place—"

"A beer can?"

"Yeah, in the bushes by the porch. The police missed it." Molly tells her mother how they took the prints off the can and then took prints off the Dodds' car. "It was parked on the street," Molly says, "so we didn't do anything illegal."

"Sheesh," Cori says, almost under her breath.

"And then we compared those with the beer can, but they didn't match. So, if we did it right—which maybe we didn't but we followed the instructions really carefully—that means it wasn't Mrs. Dodds or her son who let Doodle out." She stops and takes another deep breath.

Another pause. Cori says, "Or the beer can wasn't from the same person."

"Yeah. Or that. That's why I need your help. I wonder if I gave you the ones we got if . . . if you could check them against the ones those cops took. And if they don't match, check them against your databases. I brought the can, too, so if we really screwed it up you could let me know." She pulls out a second bag, with the beer can inside.

"Molly . . ." This time there is a really long pause before Cori speaks. Molly twirls her hair, her face drawn and anxious.

Cori sighs. "Molly, it's not like CSI or some TV show. I don't have instant access to every database. I'd have to request copies of the prints. And explain why. I can hardly say it's because my daughter is learning to do fingerprints."

Molly doesn't answer immediately. She stares ahead, her fingers working a strand of hair. "Why not?" she says at last. "They have bring-your-kid-to-work day. Why not teach-your-kid-the-job day?"

Cori snorts, shaking her head. "Okay. You win. I'll see what I can find. But if you think you want to be a detective, I suspect you're missing your true vocation."

"What?" Molly asks.

"Defense attorney!" her mother says crisply.

Chapter 18

Problem Solving

When Cori drops us off, Tanya greets us at the door. "How'd it go?" she asks eagerly.

"Great." Molly unbuckles my harness as soon as we're inside and I shake away the traces. When the girls head to Tanya's room, I stick close behind them so I don't get shut out.

"Anyone call from the shelters?" Molly asks.

Tanya shakes her head. "I don't know where he could be."

Molly settles on Tanya's bed and I take my usual spot on the floor. She doesn't speak for a minute. Then, "Benita looked awful."

"Really?" Tanya's eyes are wide with sympathy.

"Yeah. Pale and, I don't know, just sick looking. And she has to talk really slow and she slurs a lot of her words."

"I'm sorry." Tanya sits down beside her and gives her a little hug.

"But she's getting better, so that's the good news." After a moment, Molly says, "Oh, and guess what? I saw Mrs. Thomas, our landlady." She tells Tanya about meeting Mrs. Thomas in the hospital corridor. "She looks a lot better than Benita. And she invited us to come visit her if we go back."

"That'd be fun." Tanya moves over to her desk and taps some keys on her laptop. "I had an idea while you were gone. Why not do a general search for service-dog scams? I mean, people complain about everything on the Internet, right? Maybe there are others who got scammed by Kirby Banes and wrote about it."

"Oh, that's a great idea!" Molly jumps up to stand behind Tanya and look at her monitor. "Did you find him?"

"Well, no, not Kirby Banes or Dyson Banks. But I found a service-dog site—I had to register to read the comments—where someone was complaining about a Kerry Bisson. Same thing as with Jordan—the family got a dog who wasn't at all well-trained. It wasn't from LSSC, though, but a place over in Maryland. And there was no photo, so I'm not sure it's the same person, but . . ."

"Banes is camera-shy, that's for sure." Then Molly stiffens. "Wait! Kirby Banes. Dyson Banks. Kerry Bisson. What do they have in common?"

Tanya doesn't answer right away. "Two-syllable first names? The first names all contain a Y?"

"Um, yeah." Molly sounds surprised by her answer. "What else? Kirby, Dyson, Bisson?"

After a moment, Tanya shakes her head. "Beats me."

"They're all brands of vacuums!" Molly gives her a triumphant look.

"Wow. The vacuum villain! I wonder why?"

"Maybe he sells vacuums when he's not scamming people?" Molly suggests.

"Or did at some point. He thinks he's clever at any rate."

"I mean it could be coincidence." Molly stares at the computer screen. "But I don't think so."

Tanya's fingers move quickly over the laptop keys. "Searching Kerry Bisson and vacuums," she says. She and Molly bend over the screen, which changes as Tanya clicks. I'm thinking a nap might be good about now as computers aren't really my thing.

But just as I'm starting to doze, Molly says in a voice heavy with disappointment, "Kerry Bisson must be an alias, too."

"So what is his *real* name?" Tanya asks.

Molly sighs. "I'm not sure how we find out."

"If we could just figure out how to contact him," Tanya says. "Like Jordan's Mom did. Make him think we want a service dog. And when he answers, we got him."

"Maybe, but we'd need proof."

"If they could trace the answer to him, it might be enough. Once we find him, we could have Mrs. Taylor testify against him."

"But how do we find him? His spoof of the LSSC site is gone and he'd be crazy to put it up while LSSC in trying to find him."

Tanya chews on a fingernail. "We search all the local service-dog sites and look for something sketchy? Or send them emails saying we need a service dog? And we see if we get an answer from Kirby Banes or any of his other aliases."

"What if . . . ?" Molly falls silent, tilting her head much like a dog trying to understand something. She suddenly sits up straight. "You know what we need to ask? How did Mrs. Taylor find the site in the first place? Did she go directly to the LSSC website or was it some general site like—"

"Like the one I was searching!" Tanya says, excited. "What if he runs a fake site on how to find service dogs? Then he could contact perspective clients and choose which legitimate site to spoof. Use different places so he doesn't get caught."

Molly grabs her phone, taps it, and then says, "Hey, Jordan."

"Did you find him?" Jordan asks eagerly.

Molly's face falls. "Oh, no. Sorry. No news on Cooper yet, but we're still looking. But could you tell me where you found out about LSSC? Did you go straight to their site or . . ."

Jordan thinks a moment. "No. We used a site that listed a whole bunch of places, and Mama emailed them all. And Kirby Banes was one of the ones who answered."

Molly and Tanya exchange a glance and then high five.

"Do you remember the site's name?" Molly asks.

"Yeah," Jordan says bitterly. "But it won't do you any good. It's not there anymore. Just like the LSSC site."

After that, Molly and Jordan talk a little more about Cooper and then Molly says goodbye. "So the site is gone," she says.

"That one," Tanya says. "I bet it's like his names and he has several and switches them around so he doesn't get caught."

Molly looks intrigued. "And he probably doesn't keep his site up for long."

"So we search every day. Keep looking and hope one of his sites pops up. Grady could help. But . . ." Tanya thinks a minute. "what do we do if we find him?"

"We answer and tell him we need a service dog," Molly says.

"And if he replies, we get a phone number and then he can be found by tracing his phone!"

Molly frowns. "I'm not sure it would be that easy. I could ask my mom."

"If he used his phone they could for sure. People are always getting tracked by their phones."

Molly nods. "Dad says Google knows everywhere we go. Makes him angry. But what if Kirby uses his desktop? Or even a laptop. And, anyway, I think the police would need some kind of court order to do it."

Tanya taps some more on her keyboard, studies the screen, then shakes her head. "Didn't Mrs. Taylor have to sign a contract? If we could get him to come to the house and bring a contract, then the police could arrest him. We could email him, and I could be the kid who needs a service dog, since you have Doodle."

"Oooooh." Molly's eyes widen at this. Then she sighs. "We'd need an adult. He wouldn't bring a contract to a bunch of kids. Do you think your mom would do that?"

"Come to this house?" Tanya grimaces. "Maybe, but she doesn't like to do anything that might even seem a little illegal."

Molly sucks in her lips, her eyes unfocused. Her fingers start to twist a strand of hair. "Yeah. Hard to imagine her saying yes."

"I know, right?" Tanya says in a dejected voice.

Molly's eyes take on this speculative expression. "But I think I know who might. And if we can find his site and get him to answer, I think we might just be able to catch him."

Chapter 19

Homecomings

MOLLY AND I ARE SITTING ON THE FRONT PORCH OF our new house, waiting for the boss and Annie. Tanya is with us, because even though the boss is supposed to be here any minute, Mrs. Franklin didn't want Molly to wait alone.

"With all that's gone on in that house," she said, "I don't want to take any chances."

Chances of what, I have no idea. Not to mention that when I'm with Molly, she's not alone.

"Are you going to tell your Dad?" Tanya asks.

Molly, who has been holding Moxy ever since we got here, scratches the kitten behind the ears. Moxy purrs like crazy. People are always saying that cats are loners, but Moxy obviously prefers to be with people.

Molly keeps her eyes on the road. "I'm not sure. Not until we get a hit. I mean, if Kirby doesn't take the bait, no harm no foul, right?"

As usual, I have no idea what she's talking about. Hits? Harm? Foul? It's almost like she's speaking Chinese. What I do know is that Molly's been sending lots of texts over the last few days.

She and Tanya have been up to something that involves Tanya's laptop, a bunch of whispering and excitement, Grady, and, as I mentioned, lots of texts.

Molly sucks in her breath, jams the kitten into Tanya's arm, and jumps up waving.

Hey, it's our van coming down the street!

"Doodle, hush!" Molly says.

Oh. Guess I was barking.

The boss pulls into the driveway and soon everyone's hugging and laughing. Hey, what about me? I try to squeeze in between the boss and Molly.

"Doodle, off!" the boss commands, but he doesn't sound like he means it.

"He doesn't want to be left out!" Tanya says. She's standing off to the side, a huge grin plastered across her face.

After Annie and the boss have each hugged Molly and petted me, they unload their suitcases, and we all go inside.

"Warm in here!" the boss says. "But it's supposed to cool off tonight and I'll get those air conditioners up first thing tomorrow."

"Mama's on her way over with your stuff," Tanya announces, handing the kitten to Molly, who quickly puts Moxy back in the mudroom. Just as quickly, Moxy starts to yowl.

Before long, Mrs. Franklin walks in, carrying a fragrant pan that smells of hamburger, cheese, and noodles along with a spice that I don't recognize. Behind her, Tyson and Kenny carry in Molly's suitcases and the bag with my things.

"You shouldn't have," the boss says, his face creasing in delight when he sees the pan.

"It's just goulash," Mrs. Franklin says. "You don't need to be cooking your first night home."

"Well, it smells wonderful." Annie takes the pan from Mrs. Franklin and carries it to the kitchen. "Thank you!"

"And thanks for watching Molly," the boss adds. "Sorry that things didn't go exactly as planned."

"You have no idea," Mrs. Franklin says, but when the boss gives her a questioning look, she just smiles. "You know we're always glad to have her. Especially when she brings Doodle." Mrs. Franklin bends down to give me a pat. "What do you think of having a new family member, Doodle?"

I'm not sure if she means Annie, Moxy, or Chloe.

The boss gives the Franklins a short tour of the house. Tanya has been here before, of course, but Mrs. Franklin and the boys haven't.

"Very nice place," she says after they finish. "Lots of room. If a little warm." Mrs. Franklin fans her face for a second. "Which reminds me, Lamar said he and Derrin could come over after supper tonight and help you get those air conditioners up."

"Wonderful!" The boss shakes his head, his voice catching a little. "You have all been so much help!"

We follow the Franklins out to the van. Mrs. Franklin settles in the driver's seat and Tyson in the back. Kenny opens the passenger door, but then stops and goes over to the gate. "So this is the scene of the crime," he says fingering the broken chain.

"Crime?" the boss asks, his voice changing. And then he stares at the chain. "How'd that happen?"

Mrs. Franklin starts the van and Kenny hurries back and gets in.

Leaning out the window, Mrs. Franklin says, "You and Molly have a lot of catching up to do." She gives him a brief smile before backing out of the driveway.

The boss strides over to the chain and grasps the dangling end. "How'd this happen?" Whoa. He sounds angry.

"It's a long story." Molly's face colors as she glances from the boss to Annie. "We didn't want to ruin your honeymoon."

"One best told over that delicious-smelling casserole," Annie says firmly, hurrying over to take the boss's arm. "We don't want it to get cold."

With a sigh, the boss allows her to steer him toward the door. We all go back inside, and soon the casserole is on the table along with a loaf of French bread and a small plate with butter. Molly sets glasses and silverware around and then they all help themselves to the food.

"A long story?" the boss asks, after swallowing his first bite. But he doesn't seem as angry as he did outside.

Molly, also swallowing, launches into what happened the night of the wedding, how the gate was open, and Jordan found me a few blocks away.

"You didn't tell me Doodle was missing?" the boss asks, the anger creeping back into his voice.

"We found him," Molly says. "And I talked it over with Mom and she agreed that if we told you it might ruin your honeymoon. And since he was safe . . ."

The boss stares at her, fork held half-way to his mouth.

"And then we got to Mom's place and found Benita unconscious and had to call an ambulance and I had to go to Tanya's and it was really late." Molly's voice breaks.

The boss starts to say something. but then falls silent.

"So anyway, that's what we decided," she adds a little defiantly. "Because you wouldn't be able to do anything from Tennessee. And Doodle was safe. And Mom called the cops who came and took fingerprints so we did everything you could have done if you were here."

"Fingerprints!" The boss's eyes narrow. "The fingerprint kit! That's why you wanted one."

"What a hard night that must have been," Annie says sympathetically.

Molly glances at the boss, but then nods at Annie. "And I never came over here by myself—Tanya and Doodle were always with me, so I wasn't here alone. We were careful."

"And did the fingerprints tell you who cut the chain?" the boss asks.

Molly shakes her head. "Mom is still checking on them. But she's been really busy with Benita." Just then, Molly's phone beeps. She flips it open, then quickly shuts it again. She goes on to tell about her visit with Benita and discovering Mrs. Thomas had had a stroke.

"Oh, I'm sorry to hear this," the boss says. "How was she?"

"Good." Molly's phone beeps again. She jumps at the sound, frowning, but doesn't open it. "Way better than Benita. She can talk fine, and was joking and thinks she'll be home in a week. She'd like us to visit her and we can bring Doodle." Molly tells the boss and Annie how Cori got permission for me to visit patients.

While she talks, I lie on the floor with the smell of the casserole in my nose wondering if they're going to sit here all night talking. I don't get fed until after they eat, and I'm hungry. But even though no one is eating any more, no one gets up from the table.

Molly's phone beeps again.

"Someone's trying to get hold of you," Annie says, pushing her plate away.

Molly's face colors. "Just Grady. It's not important."

Hard to believe given the tension in her voice.

And then her phone plays the tune that means someone is calling. With a ferocious frown, she flips it open. Her frown fades.

"Hello?" she asks somewhat tentatively.

"Molly Hunter?" a high voice asks. "Celia Stewart. I owned the dog—"

"Yes!" Molly says, "Jack! Who's now called Cooper!"

"Yeah! Hey, I got a call from a shelter in Arlington saying they found him."

Eyes aglow, Molly mouths to the boss and Annie, "They found Cooper!" She makes a motion in the air like she's writing.

"That's wonderful! We've been looking everywhere for him. Can you give me the name of the shelter? Wait. One second." She gives the boss an imploring look.

He jumps up, pulls a pen and small tablet from a draw at the end of counter and slides them over to Molly.

"Okay, I'm ready." She listens and writes. "Great. I'll call them right away. Thanks so much!"

"Yeah. But could you get the info changed? So I don't keep getting the calls?"

Molly flushes. "Sure. I mean I thought the owners had already done it, but I'll remind them." She says goodbye and closes her phone.

"Cooper was missing?" Annie asks.

Molly nods. "He ran away during this big thunderstorm. He got really scared. And we've been calling shelters and searching everywhere for him." She opens her phone again. "I've got to tell Jordan!"

"Is there anything that *didn't* happen while we were gone?" the boss asks, his voice soft and incredulous.

The doorbell rings. I give a low bark, leaping to my feet.

"And we seem to be living in Grand Central Station," the boss murmurs, rising to his feet. But he breaks into a smile when he opens the door and sees Mr. Franklin and Derrin.

After giving them a polite greeting and getting a few pats, I go back to the kitchen. Molly and Annie are *still* sitting at the table. Seriously? Can I mention here that dogs don't believe in lingering over a meal? Get the job done and move on is our motto. I go over to Molly, sit in front of her and stare.

"I think someone is hungry," Annie says, smiling. She rises—at last!—and Molly gets up and opens the tall cupboard by the door where my kibble is kept. She scoops the usual amount into my dish. I had hopes for some casserole, but Molly, seeing me glance at the dish that's still on the table, says, "Sorry. It has a lot of onions and garlic."

I have my opinions on foods that are supposedly "bad for dogs" but I'm hungry enough that the kibble tastes pretty good. As I'm crunching it down—I'm not the swallow-it-whole type like some dogs—Molly's phone rings again.

"Hey, Mrs. Taylor," she says happily, but her smile fades as she listens. I can't hear what Jordan's mother is saying over the noise of chewing my food, and I have my priorities.

"Okay," Molly says in a small voice. "But we could try to train—" more talking on the other end. "Okay," she says again. "We'll figure out something." She glances over at Annie, who is rinsing dishes and putting them in the drainer. "Okay." And then she hangs up.

"Mrs. Jordan says she doesn't want Cooper back!" Molly says, clearly upset.

"Oh, no!" Annie's eyes are dark with sympathy. "But why?"

"She says Cooper has been nothing but trouble since the day they got him and that Cooper was supposed to help Jordan watch his blood sugar, but instead he's caused so much stress for them that Jordan's blood sugar has been all over the map. He's doing more harm than good."

Annie places a bowl in the drainer and turns off the water. "I can see how she would feel that," she says at last. "Like I said before, I wondered if he's the right dog for that family."

"You could train him to be the right dog," Molly blurts. "It might take a lot of time, but—" She flops into a chair, staring at the table. I go over to her and put my head in her lap. "Jordan *loves* him."

"If you are 5'2" and weigh 125 pounds do you think you have the prospects of being a pro basketball player?" Annie asks gently. "No matter how much you practice?"

Molly doesn't answer.

"Like humans, dogs have different genetic strengths and capacities. Many of these can be enhanced by training, but even so, the drop-out rate of dogs bred to be service dogs can be 50–75 percent. Some service-dog jobs are harder than others, of course. A seeing-eye dog has a higher level of training than a diabetic alert dog, because it has to negotiate obstacles and traffic that a blind person can't see. But at the very least, a diabetic alert dog has to be committed to his charge, be able to distinguish the scent of changing blood sugar and be well-behaved in public."

Molly strokes my head, still not looking up.

"I can train him to be good in public, but I might spend all the time in the world with him and still not achieve the other two. I *might*, but there's no guarantee. And that's scary when someone's life could be on the line."

"So what about Cooper? We can't just leave him in the shelter!" Molly looks up for the first time. "Maybe we could adopt him."

Annie seems alarmed by this suggestion. "How about this? I'll go down tomorrow and get him from the shelter and take him out to Miguel's. I have to go out there anyway to pick up Chloe. And I'll board him there and work with him and see where his strengths are. It's better to pick a job for him that suits his skills."

Molly brightens at this. After a long pause, she says, "I guess maybe he's kind of like Snippet, who really didn't want to be a bed bug dog even with all your training."

Annie says, "Exactly," and goes over and hugs her.

I go back to lick my bowl in case I missed something, while Molly calls the shelter and tells them Annie will pick up Cooper in the morning. Then I put my nose to the mudroom door my signal that I need to go out. Molly carefully eases it open, her foot in place to block Moxy from running in.

But Moxy isn't in the mudroom. No wonder we haven't heard her complaining.

"Where is she?" Molly asks, hurrying through the backyard door calling, "Here kitty-kitty! Here kitty-kitty!" She scans the yard. "Here kitty-kitty." Under her breath, she mutters, "Please don't be lost."

And then an unmistakable meowing starts up over by the trees. Not by the trees, it turns out, but high up *in* one of the trees. As we watch, Moxy carefully works her way down the trunk and drops to the ground.

"Look at you!" Molly says. "Learning new things!" She swoops up the kitten and settles in one of the lawn chairs. "What a day!"

For a few minutes, she just sits there and pets a now-purring Moxy. I make my rounds around the fence, checking for intruders. When I come back and shove my nose in her lap, she laughs, and then, more soberly, pulls out her phone.

"One more thing to do," she says. And then, "Hey, Grady. Sorry I couldn't answer your texts. Dad and Annie came home, and we were all sitting at the table."

Grady sounds upset. "So you're not telling them?"

"Well . . . is it on?" Molly asks. "I had like a million things to tell them since they've been gone, and I didn't want Dad to have a fit."

"Mama just made the appointment an hour ago. So it's on."

Molly says, "Wow. It worked! He took the bait."

"I know. Mama's practically beside herself she's so excited. What about your mom? Did you ask her?"

"Not yet," Molly says. "I didn't want to unless we knew it was going to happen for sure."

Grady sounds impatient. "Molly, this was your idea. She's a key part. We don't want it to fall through. Mama will be madder than a hornet."

"I know. I won't," Molly promises. "I'll call her right away."

She says goodbye to Grady, sucks in a big breath and lets it out slowly. "Here goes nothing." She taps her phone.

"Molly." Cori answers almost immediately. "I was just thinking about you. Benita's doing better. The doc thinks maybe three or four more days and she can come home."

"That's great!" Molly looks pleased, in spite of the tension I smell coming from her. She and her mother talk about Benita for a few moments and then, after a ragged breath, Molly says, "I had an idea about how we could catch Kirby Banes."

"Who?" her mother asks.

"The guy who sold the fake service dog to my friend, Jordan? You met him the night Jordan found Doodle."

"Oh, yeah. Did you know there was a big case over in North Carolina? Some guy was accused of selling service dogs that were horrible—not housebroken, attacked other dogs."

"Yeah," Molly says, her voice even tighter. "I read about that. In Illinois and Colorado, too. But—" she gulps "—about this guy. I wonder if you could help us catch him."

"It's not my jurisdiction," Cori begins, "and I—"

Molly interrupts. "Couldn't you like coordinate it with the Arlington cops? We have this great idea of how to get him, but we need you there. You remember Madison? Grady's mom?"

At that moment, the door opens, and Annie lets Chloe out. She grabs an old glove, one of her toys, and races past me. Of course I have to chase her.

We're still playing when I see Molly heading for the door, so naturally I quit the game and run to her side. Her phone, no longer at her ear, buzzes in her pocket. She stops and flips it open. "Grady," she says. "I called her. It's a go."

But Grady doesn't sound happy. "Mama just told me you have to tell your dad, or you can't come over. She won't do it without his permission."

Molly's face falls. "Okay. I'll ask. I mean I don't technically have to be there, but—"

"It would be better with you and Doodle. It's what we planned."

"I know. I really want to be there." She swallows. "I'll ask him right now." And then, closing her phone, she goes through the door and repeats, "Here goes nothing."

Chapter 20

Undercover

We're sitting on the porch of our new house waiting for Cori. Molly is as nervous as one of those little dogs I see shivering at the vet's. She's been twisting a strand of hair since she dropped anxiously into one of the lawn chairs, and the boss isn't much better. He strokes his beard, plops down briefly beside her, only to bounce back up and pace the length of the porch.

"I hope this isn't a huge mistake," he repeats. He's been saying this a lot.

"It'll be perfectly safe," Molly answers. "Mom will be there. She knows what she's doing. And Madison has done this kind of thing before. It's not like he's an armed robber or anything."

The boss grimaces.

"Plus, I have Doodle. He won't let anything happen to me."

She's right about that, but it would help if I knew what she was talking about. I look up and down the street. Nothing unusual. A car come towards us, but I quickly recognize it as Cori's.

As it turns into our driveway, the boss pulls Molly into a fierce hug. "Don't take any risks," he says, his voice thick.

"I won't," she promises. And then, she says, "Come on, Doodle," and leads me over to Cori's car, putting me in the back seat.

The boss watches us as we back out of the driveway and onto the road.

We ride in silence, the only talking coming from Cori's phone telling us where to go. After what seems like a long time, Molly straightens up.

"That's it," she says, pointing. "The one with the big garage."

"I hope this works," Cori says, sounding much like the boss.

Oddly, she doesn't pull into the broad driveway in front of Grady's home, but parks half a block down the street. Molly snaps on my leash, gets me out, and we all walk back. Grady is waiting for us, door open, as we turn into the driveway.

"Hey," he says, glancing anxiously up and down the street. As if he's afraid of something. He motions us inside. Is he expecting intruders? He's as nervous as Molly—I can smell it on him, and I'm beginning to wonder what's wrong. It's hard to stay calm with all the tension in the air. Makes me want to bark. I scratch my ear.

"Mama's got the camera set up. She'll be down in a second." He waves a hand at the stairs on the far side of the room.

Molly sinks down into one of the plush chairs beside the couch and I lie at her feet. Cori remains standing, studying the room.

Then Madison bustles down the stairs. She's dressed in her usual tight pants and flowing blouse, and she smells like hair spray and soap. And nerves. Everyone here is nervous and not in a happy, expecting-something-good kind of way.

Madison goes over to Cori. "Thank you for coming," she says. "I can't tell you how much it relieves my mind to have you here."

"Well." Cori's mouth twists. "Not sure if I should be or not, but—" she glances at Molly "—my daughter is very persuasive."

Madison gestures to the dining room. "You can wait in here," she says. "Around the corner, where you can hear but won't be seen. I pulled a chair over for you."

Cori follows her into the other room and disappears for a second, and then comes back and sits beside Molly. Madison perches on an armchair, plucking at a bit of dog hair from the cushion. Come to think of it, I wonder where Snippet is. Usually she's always right beside Grady.

"What did you do with Snippet?" Molly asks.

"At the groomer's," Madison answers. "And Grady vacuumed for a long time, but it's hard to get every bit of hair."

"Vacuums!" Molly says. "Maybe Mr. Kirby/Dyson/Bisson can give you a recommendation." Both Cori and Madison smile at this.

Outside, I hear a car pull into the driveway, and then footsteps approaching the door. I watch the door, alert, ready to bark if needed. The doorbell rings. Molly and Grady jump.

Cori slips into the other room. Madison looks over at Grady. "Ready?" she mouths. He nods.

The hair rises on my back. They're all acting like this is going be an intruder.

But when Madison pulls open the door, it is with a big smile. "Come on in," she says in that sugary voice she sometimes uses, the one thick with what the boss calls a "southern accent."

A dark-haired man around the same age as the boss steps through the door. He's nicely dressed in slacks and a short-sleeved shirt with a tie, and has dark shiny shoes. He flashes a big smile at Madison. Wait a minute. I recognize him! He's the man Molly took photos of at the grooming place.

He offers a hand. "Bryan Shark," he says.

Molly sucks in her breath and glances at Grady, twitching her mouth into a tiny, brief smile. He gives an almost imperceptible nod back.

Madison takes his hand, her eyes lowered slightly in what the boss calls her flirtatious look. "I'm Madison and that—" she tilts her head toward Grady "—is my son Grady. And his friend, Molly with her service dog, Doodle."

What? *Service* dog?

"Please, take a seat, Mr. Shark," Madison says.

He chooses the armchair that faces Grady and Molly. "Bryan, please," he says crossing his legs.

Madison sits in a chair next to him. "Molly's the one who gave me the idea of checking out Always There Service Dogs. Doodle has been such a help to her, hasn't he, honey?"

For some reason, Molly nods, even though, as far as I can tell, Madison is talking nonsense. Madison lowers her voice a bit and says, "Molly has seizures, poor baby. But since she's had Doodle, her life has been *much* better."

Seizures? I'm totally lost!

Molly reaches down to pat my head. And then, almost sounding near tears, "I don't know what I'd do without Doodle!"

That at least makes sense.

"It's amazing the difference a dog can make in a child's life." Bryan's voice brims with understanding. He leans toward Grady. "We'll just have to get you your own, won't we?"

"I like hearing that," Madison says a little tartly, "but when I called the Always There people, I was told they have a minimum two-year waiting list. Grady ended up in the emergency room with a blood sugar crash, and—" she shakes her head, giving the man an anguished look. "I just don't want to take the chance that that could happen again."

Bryan nods. With a gushing sincerity that reminds me of some of the TV preachers my second boss (don't get me started) used to watch, he says, "I understand completely. It's for people like you—with children like Grady here who need a dog right away—that we've developed the Express Always There plan. With the Express program, we could get your son a dog much like—" he inclines an arm in my direction "—this wonderful dog here, in just a month or two."

He spreads his arms, palms up. "I won't lie to you. This program isn't free. It isn't cheap. Training a qualified, certified service dog costs a lot of money. That's why ATSD spends so much time and effort fundraising. Which is wonderful—they definitely fill a need, especially for families who otherwise might never afford a dog—but it can also leave someone like yourself—someone with an urgent, *immediate* need—out in the cold."

"How expensive?" Madison asks, sitting forward in her chair.

"Around fifteen thousand dollars." He gives a deep sigh. "A lot of money, I know. "You're lucky you don't need a seizure-alert dog. They can be even more expensive because only a few dogs can actually successfully predict an oncoming seizure." He flashes a smile at Molly. "Am I right, young lady?"

Molly stiffens. "I'm not sure," she says, sounding flustered. "We, um, we got Doodle for free. But we had to wait a long time. My dad was really worried."

What? Once again Molly's making stuff up. I can't figure out why.

"So," he says, nodding at Molly and then turning back to Madison, "you might want to apply for the free program and hope that . . . well, hope that Grady here will do okay until you're able to get a dog."

"What do we have to do to qualify for the Express program?" Madison asks briskly.

Bryan bends down, opens his briefcase, and takes out some papers. "It's an easy process—much simpler than the regular program which requires a doctor's certificate, affidavits and so on. Fill out these out—there are two copies of the contract, one for you and one for me—sign them, put down a deposit, and you'll be on your way."

He gives me a speculative look. "I have a poodle in the last stages of training that looks much like this dog here, except it has a red coat."

"Red!" Grady says enthusiastically. "I love red dogs!"

Molly lowers her head. Before she puts her hand over her mouth, I see a tiny smile.

Madison frowns. "And does that include support for us to know how to handle the dog, what to expect, and all that?"

"Absolutely! We're known for our caring support of all our clients. If you go to our website, you can read the testimonials."

Madison doesn't answer for a minute. She has the unfocused look of someone thinking hard. Then, decisively, she looks the man in the eye. "Let's do it!"

He hands her the papers along with a pen. After a quick scan of the pages, Madison pulls a book from the coffee table to her lap and begins to write.

"How long have you had, um, is it Diddle?" Bryan asks Molly.

"Doodle," Molly answers. "About two years. It's really made a difference."

"I can imagine," Bryan says, his voice warm and sympathetic.

"This red poodle," Grady asks eagerly, "is it a male or female?"

"A female about a year and half old," the man says. "Very sweet natured."

Molly and Grady exchange a look—the kind that means something, although what I couldn't begin to guess what.

"Sounds like the perfect dog for you," Molly says.

Seriously? Grady has Snippet, who has a red coat and is sweet-natured and is already the perfect dog for him.

After a few minutes, Madison puts her pen and book back on the table. "Done!" She hands the papers to Bryan.

"Perfect," he says, with another large smile. "I'll just sign both copies here." He signs the papers and hands one set back to her. "Here's your copy."

"How much is the deposit?" Madison asks.

"Ten percent now, which will be $1,500, then the balance on the day I deliver the dog."

"And who do I make it out to?"

"LSSC Express," he says.

Madison rises. "I'll get my checkbook." She goes through the dining room and disappears briefly into the kitchen. She returns holding a check and with a little flourish, holds it out to him. Pockeing the check, he moves closer to grasp her hand.

"Welcome to LSSC Express!"

At that moment, the front door bursts open. Startled, I bark. A uniformed policeman strides straight toward us.

With a sudden panicked expression, Bryan bounds toward the dining room but stops dead when Cori appears in the doorway, blocking him.

He whirls around, almost crashing into the officer now right behind him.

"Bryan Shark," Cori says in a ringing, authoritative voice, "I am arresting you for fraud. You have the right to remain silent and to refuse to answer questions. Anything you say may be used against you in a court of law. You have the right to consult an attorney—"

Bryan, his face now contorted in anger, lets out a stream of words the boss would call "language" ending with "I want an attorney. This is entrapment."

"I don't think so," Cori says crisply. "But you certainly can have an attorney. You can call one down at the station."

She and the other policeman escort him through the front door. Molly and I follow and watch as they put Bryan in the backseat of a police car, its lights flashing.

Madison, standing behind us, says, "I think that went well. You kids were quite convincing. If I ever need undercover operatives again, I'll know who to call."

Undercover? Molly was undercover? So *that's* what was happening? Who knew? I think I might have mentioned that I went undercover once. It turns out to have nothing to do with blankets and everything to do with pretending to be someone you're not.

Molly beams at Madison. "Grady was great, too. So excited about a red female dog!"

They grin at each other. Then, Molly tugs her phone from her pocket and taps it.

"Are you okay?" Hey, it's the boss's voice.

"It worked!" Molly says triumphantly. "He's in custody."

"Good," the boss says, sounding more relieved than happy. "I've been sitting here wondering why I let you talk me into this. But you're okay?"

"I'm great," she answers. "We're all fine. Everything is great. We got him."

Chapter 21
Surprise Beginning

We're back at the hospital, my nails clicking on the shiny floors that stretch down long halls.

"I don't know why she asked us to come a few hours before Denzel," the boss says, setting a brisk pace.

"Maybe just to avoid a scene?" Annie suggests. "Didn't you say he was really rude when he found we were renting the house?"

The boss nods. "Rude isn't half of it. I just worry that maybe she's changed her mind. If we have to move again . . ."

"I bet Annie's right," Molly's voice is firm. "Doesn't want a scene in the hospital."

The boss slows down and squints at a closed door we're passing. "But a stroke might have changed her perspective. Made her think family was more important. I just—oh, 241. Here we are."

We turn into a room much like the one we saw when we visited Benita. This one is a little bigger, with extra chairs. Smells much the same, though, except for the human scents.

Mrs. Thomas is sitting up in bed. On the stand beside her is a large cup, along with a couple of books, some papers, and several pens. The boss and Annie go up to her, the boss with a strained smile on his face. "This is my wife, Annie—" he puts an arm around Annie "—and this is Margaret Thomas, our landlady."

Mrs. Thomas reaches over and takes Annie's hand. "So nice to meet you," she says in a strong voice. And then her gaze turns to Molly and me. "And there they are. Our undercover heroes!" She glances back at the boss. "I'm a huge fan of Madison's Low Down News. That was quite a story."

Molly grins, looking a little embarrassed. "I didn't think she'd include some video of me and Doodle," she says.

"Well, you and Doodle made great undercover agents. I bet Doodle was surprised to find out he was a service dog instead of a bed bug dog."

That's for sure. Had me confused.

"But you all played your parts very convincingly." Mrs. Thomas winks at Molly. "You might have an acting career ahead of you."

Molly flushes. "Grady told me his mom had more views on that vlog than on any for the last few years."

Mrs. Thomas nods. "I believe it. It's gratifying to see men like Shark get caught for preying on innocent people. I felt so sorry for Jordan and his family!"

Annie says, "It was awful. But they're doing well now. The people at Life Support Service Canines have stepped forward—probably from all the bad publicity—and are giving Jordan a service dog. A real one that has been thoroughly trained."

"I'm delighted to hear this," Mrs. Thomas says.

The boss clears his throat. "And how are you doing?" he asks her.

"Good! I get out of this place in two days!" She points at the chairs by the window. "You're welcome to sit down. I had the nurses bring in a couple of extra for today."

The boss, Annie, and Molly all take seats. The boss, his shoulders stiff and his mouth drawn tight, looks uncomfortable. I lie down at Molly's feet, sniffing under the bed.

Mrs. Thomas turns to Molly. "And your aunt? How is she doing?"

"Better," Molly says. "She went home the night before last. But she's still going to need a lot of therapy and stuff."

"I hear you," she says. "I have the next few months booked with appointments."

There's a pause, and then Mrs. Thomas says, "You're probably wondering why I asked you to come."

The boss nods, rubbing his beard. Annie pushes back a strand of hair.

"I've been doing a lot of thinking while I've been cooped up here. About, well, my legacy. What I want to leave when I die."

The boss sucks in a breath and holds it.

"It's foolish to think you can control anything after your death, but I want to at least try to influence the ways some things go. I don't want that lovely home that you're in to be torn down and turned into apartments. And that's what will happen if my son inherits it." She pauses a second. "I want to sell it to you."

The boss slowly exhales, leaning forward, his mouth open. Annie's eyes widen.

Mrs. Thomas shakes her head. "I have so many memories there. Mercy! So many. And those trees. Those lovely, beautiful trees. A developer would chop them down in a heartbeat."

The boss stares at her, not moving, not saying a word.

"So," Mrs. Thomas taps the stack of papers on the table beside her, "I decided to get all my ducks in a row."

Ducks? Lost me there. I raise my nose and sniff. Nothing.

"And do it while I still can be classified as mentally capable so there's no wiggle room for the contract to be invalidated. I had my attorney come and testify that I'm of sound mind, and I've revised my will. I'm not cutting Denzel out by any means—" her face darkens "—although I probably ought to. What I'd like to do is sell you the place. If you want to finance it, you can, or we can do it with seller financing, and I will give you a competitive interest rate. Either way, I will have a monthly sum go to Denzel. I think that will be healthier for him than a lump sum. I'd want a clause that you won't resell the property for at least five years." She gives us a crooked smile. "Just so I can tell Denzel that I'm not being played for a fool." Her voice hardens a bit. "Which I would be if you turned around and sold it."

The boss clears his throat. "We love that house. I wouldn't sell it." He turns to Annie who is nodding vigorously.

"I wouldn't either. I love it," she says.

"This all sounds . . . wonderful." The boss clears his throat again. "But—how much will you be asking? I'm not sure if we can afford it."

"That's why I asked you here. I thought we could discuss what you think you could pay and still be able to keep Doodle here—" she grins at me "—in dogfood."

The boss and Annie, both looking suddenly energized, exchange a look. He takes out his phone. But he doesn't make a call but taps a bunch of keys, biting his lower lip, his forehead creased.

Annie stands up. "I wonder if we might—if you could excuse us for a few minutes so we could discuss it."

The boss, rising, says, "That's a great idea. I need to make a few calls."

"Of course," Mrs. Thomas says, smiling. "Molly here can tell me what it's like to catch criminals."

The boss and Annie hurry out to the lobby.

Mrs. Thomas and Molly talk, but not about criminals. Molly tells her how she and Tanya met and how they're best friends and go to school together.

"I love the Franklins," Mrs. Thomas says. "Salt of the earth people. We need more like them." They go on like this, so I take a little nap, my head down on the shiny floor, the scent of disinfectant in my nose.

When the boss comes back, he looks considerably more cheerful. "I talked to my parents and Annie to her mother, and think we might be able to make it work if we had a down payment we could afford and could keep the payment within a hundred dollars of our current rent," he says.

Mrs. Thomas smiles, her face lighting up. "I think we can do that." She hands him a stack of papers. "Read through this and see if you can agree to the terms. I left the price of the home and down payment blank, but we can insert it. If you're willing to go ahead, I have a notary who can be here in fifteen minutes."

The boss looks at her in surprise. "Wouldn't it be easier to wait until you got home?" he asks.

Now Mrs. Thomas's smile fades. "Maybe, but I don't want to take the chance. While I hope to live another twenty years just to annoy Denzel, two people in this rehab have had a second stroke within the last week. Out of blue. Just as they were getting ready to go home. I want to sew this up while I can."

She turns, gazing out the window for a moment. Then, with a sigh, she says, "I guess I can tell you—but please keep it confidential. Denzel is pushing me to sign a power of attorney. Not that I'd do that in a million years. He keeps saying since I've had a stroke, I shouldn't handle my finances. I want to wrap this up right now while there's no question that I'm mentally capable of doing so."

The boss gives her a sympathetic look. "I understand. I'm sorry." He pauses. "I wondered why you were rushing this through. But that makes sense." He picks up the papers and begins to read, holding them so Annie sees them as well.

Molly checks her phone and sends some texts. I consider another nap. The boss looks up after a few minutes. He and Annie exchange another look, the boss nodding at her raised eyebrows.

"Looks fine to us," Annie says. "If we can agree on price, you can call the notary."

They talk for a bit, a conversation hard to follow as it involves a lot of numbers and words like down payments and interest, something I'm not really into. But when they finish and Annie and the boss go over to the bed and shake hands with Mrs. Thomas, I understand the emotion. Excitement and happiness. The boss, his shoulders relaxed now, gives Annie a big hug while Mrs. Thomas makes a phone call.

Annie says, "I think I'm going to find the vending machines Anyone want anything?"

These kinds of questions are never directed at me, alas, but Molly jumps up and says. "I'll go with you." Naturally, I want to go as well, but Molly hands my leash to the boss, and she and Annie take off.

Mrs. Thomas leans against the bed and closes her eyes. "Think I'll rest just for a moment."

"Sure," the boss says. He checks his phone and I doze until Molly and Annie come back, wrappers crackling in their hands.

"We got sweet and salty." Annie drops some candy bars and a few bags of chips on the bed. She starts to divide them but stops when a stout woman with short hair and feet bulging through tight sandals walks briskly into the room.

Mrs. Thomas introduces her, but I'm captivated by the scent coming from one of the woman's sandals. It's faint, but there's a definite odor of bird poop from the bottom of the shoe.

None of the humans notice, of course. The adults are busy signing papers and Molly has her head bent over her phone.

When they all finish, Mrs. Thomas hands the woman some money, which she takes with a smile, and walks toward the door as briskly as she came in. She almost collides with a man barreling around the corner.

"Excuse me," the man says, pushing past her. Then he stops dead and turns back. "What are you doing here?" he asks the woman, followed by an accusing glance at Mrs. Thomas. "Mama, why is *she* here?"

Wait. I recognize the scent! The intruder who opened the gate. I will never forget it. My hair rises on my back and I find I'm growling.

"Doodle!" Molly whispers, alarmed.

I stop growling but keep my eyes on him. No one is treating him like an intruder, but I know that he is.

"Why is she here?" he demands in a voice angry enough to make me growl again.

Molly yanks my leash a little. "Down!" she commands in a low voice.

I don't want to go down. I want to sit where I can watch this man more easily. I ignore the command. The man glares at me, and it's all I can do not to growl again.

Mrs. Thomas seems unaware of all the emotion in the room. She waves at the man cheerfully. "Hi, Denzel. Ms. Young is just leaving." She gestures to the boss and Annie. "You remember my son, Denzel."

Denzel stalks over to his mother's bed on the opposite side of where we are. I keep my eyes on him, ready for action.

"What was she doing here?" he demands again. Beads of sweat dot his forehead.

Mrs. Thomas says placidly, "She was here to notarize the sale of the Verdun Street house to these good folks here."

"*What?* You *sold* it?" He shakes his head, incredulous. "How? Why?"

Mrs. Thomas leans forward. "Because I decided to," she snaps. "And it's my property."

"It's our *family* property, Mama, and I should have a say as to what happens to it."

Now Mrs. Thomas shakes her head. "Son, I don't know where you get that. You didn't make the mortgage payments for twenty years on this place, skimping sometimes in order to do it. You didn't work extra shifts like your daddy did or take in secretarial work like I did to pay for it. You got an eighteen-year vacation in this home. You don't own a red cent of it."

For a moment, Denzel doesn't speak, his face darkening. "It won't hold up," he says at last, angrily. "Whatever you've done won't hold up in court. You've had a stroke. You shouldn't be doing this kind of stuff, Mama. You got to believe me that I only want what's best for you."

Mrs. Thomas shakes her head, and her face turns sad. "Oh, Denzel, how I wish I could believe that. Lord, how I wish that."

"It true!" he blusters. "You shouldn't have to worry about these things at your age."

"At my age," she says with a considerable edge to her voice, "I don't want to worry about my son running through all my savings in nothing flat."

He doesn't seem to hear her. Leaning over the bed toward us, he says in a low hard voice, much like a growl. "It's all your doing. Undue influence over a woman in the hospital."

I don't like his tone or his threatening stance at all. I growl back.

"*Doodle!*" the boss says, angry himself. Molly gives a quick tug on the leash.

But Mrs. Thomas surprises me. She laughs, shaking her head. Although somehow her eyes still hold some sadness. "Oh, son, you know that won't fly. I've spoken to my lawyer. Give up on it. And remember this is one property. You'll still inherit the Falls Church rentals as well as the payments and interest on this property."

Another silence. At last, Denzel sighs, and some of the anger seems to leave him. "Fine," he says, his voice sullen now. "Have it your way." And without another word, he stalks out of room.

"I'm sorry you had to hear that," Mrs. Thomas says. "But I thought . . . well, now you understand why I decided to sell."

Chapter 22

Happy Endings

WE'RE GETTING READY FOR OUR FIRST PARTY IN OUR new home. Well, at least the humans are. Chloe and I are sacked out under the big trees resting after a great game of chase.

Annie calls this a house-warming party, although that doesn't make sense as the boss runs air conditioners to keep the house cool.

The boss found this new picnic table "for a steal" even though I saw him pay for it, and had it delivered earlier today. Now, sporting a vinyl tablecloth, it holds paper plates and cups and a variety of condiments. The boss has his grill fired up and a tray of hamburger patties and hot dogs—not really *dogs*, of course—ready to cook.

"How many are coming?" he asks Annie, who is carrying a big pitcher of water to a side table brought out from the house.

Annie pushes her hair back from her face. "The Franklins, Madison and Grady, Jordan and Keira, and . . . I think that's it. Thirteen including us. I invited Miguel and Rosa, but he begged off. And—" she turns to Molly, busily arranging plastic silverware into large cups "—your mom isn't coming, right?"

Molly bites her lower lip. "She doesn't think Benita is up to it yet and she doesn't want to leave her alone. And . . ." Molly frowns a little, looking suddenly uncomfortable. "I think it's—"

"Awkward for her?" Annie finishes. "I can understand that. It would be for me. I just didn't want her to feel left out, especially since she was instrumental in catching Kirby."

"And the only reason I let you be there!" the boss says fervently. "Still not sure that was a wise decision."

"It was never dangerous," Molly insists. She and the boss have had this conversation before.

When the Franklins arrive, they come carrying several fragrant dishes. "Potato salad," Mrs. Franklin announces, setting a large bowl on the table. "Baked beans. And peach pies," she adds as Kenny and Tanya set several smaller dishes down. Derrin's carrying a softball and several mitts, and soon he and Kenny and Tyson are playing catch on the other side of the trees. Tanya goes straight to Molly, of course, and then to the mudroom where Moxy is hiding out. She returns with a purring Moxy in her arms.

Mr. Franklin heads to the grill to help the boss. The meat sizzles and the wafting smoke fills my nose with mouth-watering scents. Literally. Chloe gets up and goes over to sit and stare at cooking meat, a thin line of drool stretching down from her mouth.

It smells wonderful, but even so I'm not as obsessed with food as Chloe is. Annie claims it's a beagle thing. All I know is that if there's food around, Chloe thinks of nothing else.

Everyone is talking, Chloe's zeroed in on the grill, and I'm semi-napping when Jordan and his mother arrive. Correction. Jordan, his mother, and a *dog* arrive. Not Cooper. A new dog. I jump up and trot over to investigate.

When I get closer, I can smell the dog is a female, and see that she's a Golden retriever, smaller than Cooper. And certainly better behaved. She walks calmly at Jordan's side, her attention on him.

"You got her!" Molly exclaims, rushing up to grab my collar just as I'm about to sniff noses with her. Tanya and Grady hurry over as well.

Jordan nods, a shy smile on his face. "Meet Lucy. I just got her a week ago. She's really sweet." He glances at me. "You can let Doodle meet her. She doesn't mind."

Molly releases me and Lucy and I sniff each other politely. Chloe's still watching the grill.

"Ow!" Tanya exclaims. Moxy's claws have come out at the sight of the dog. Tanya drops her on the ground and the kitten dashes around her and straight up the nearest tree. Cats!

Lucy lifts her head, ears raised, and watches Moxy, but doesn't move from Jordan's side.

"She scratched me!" Tanya shows Molly the thin lines of blood on her arm.

"It's her first party ever," Molly says apologetically. "She's never seen this many people in her life."

Well, maybe, but clearly none of these people mean any harm. But that's the thing about cats. They see danger everywhere. If a dog left marks like that on a person's arm, he'd be in big trouble, but somehow a cat can get away with it. Just sayin' . . .

"Did you see that?" Keira says proudly, bending down to lightly touch Lucy's head. "She didn't budge when that cat ran. She's so well-trained." She turns to Annie. "You kept telling me that Cooper wasn't and I knew he wasn't, but now with Lucy I *really* know what you mean. She's so good. So reliable! She's already alerted on one of Jordan's blood sugar drops—two days after we got her! It's such a relief to be able to trust her. I can go to work without worrying."

Now that I think about it, Keira looks more relaxed than I've ever seen her.

Jordan's face clouds momentarily. "Cooper was a good dog," he says a little defensively. "Mostly." He sighs, and Lucy nudges his hand, her nose working. All her attention is on him.

"Cooper has a great heart," Annie agrees. "I've been working with him every day and he's made a lot of progress. He really wants to please. Unfortunately, I think he's always going be afraid of thunderstorms, which rules him out from most service-dog jobs and right now he's a little high energy for a therapy dog, but I think when he's older he might be a perfect candidate for that."

"Meanwhile—" She gives Jordan a glowing smile. "I think I've found the perfect home for him. I have a friend who recently lost her dog to cancer. She trains agility dogs so Cooper will get plenty of exercise and she has twin girls who are nine who will keep him busy. I think it'll be a perfect fit."

A mixture of relief and happiness floods Jordan's face. "Oh," he says. "That's terrific. I know he had problems but . . ."

"You cared for him! Naturally!" Annie gives him an understanding smile. "Don't worry! They're going to pick him up next week. And if for some reason it doesn't work out, they'll return him to me. I always insist on that when I rehome dogs. I won't let him end up in a shelter."

I hear another van pull into the driveway and recognize it immediately. Soon, Madison sashays through the gate, a sheet cake in hand. The boss likes to say that she always acts like she's the beauty queen in the parade, something I don't quite understand. But everyone seems happy to see her. Annie takes the cake from her with a smile. No chance of my getting any since it's chocolate. Grady follows, his arms sagging under the weight of plastic bottles of soda topped with a couple of bags of chips.

"Why isn't this just as cute as a button?" Madison says, surveying the yard. "I didn't realize this was so big. Nice." She's wearing sparkling sandals, tight shorts, and a flowing blouse and for once has her hair pulled back under a broad-brimmed hat. "I wish we had trees like that. Ours are puny little things."

Keira beelines over to her. "Thank you so *so* much for that piece you did about us. Come see who we have!" She waves an arm proudly at Lucy.

While Madison is admiring Lucy, Grady sets his armload down on the table and Molly and Tanya carry the sodas to the drink table.

Soon people are filling glasses and making their way to the picnic table. The boss and Mr. Franklin bring over trays with the burgers and hot dogs and everyone fills their plate, all talking a mile a minute.

The table doesn't quite fit everyone, and the boss and Mr. Franklin use kitchen chairs at the end corners, while the Franklin boys sit on lawn chairs nearby, balancing plates of food on their laps. Always a promising situation, and I watch for spills out of the corner of my eye.

And then, people are murmuring how good it all looks, followed by a brief silence as they fill their mouths. I lie by Molly's feet. She's usually good to give me bits from her plate when the boss isn't looking. I know enough not to beg, though. She never gives me food if I'm begging. I'm not sure Chloe understands that as she's sitting, watching the table with an intensity of a cat staring at a bird, an even bigger line of drool dropping from her mouth.

Speaking of cats, Moxy, evidently deciding her life wasn't in danger, allowed Grady to pry her from the tree and is now purring on his lap. Lucy lies at Jordan's feet, not showing any interest in the food at all.

Mrs. Franklin washes down a mouthful with a swallow of lemonade and then turns to Madison. "I'd never watched a—what do you call it?—*vlog* before, but my boys showed me how to set it up on our TV and I have to say you've made me a believer. And not just because you gave these girls here—" she glances at Molly and Tanya, her eyes twinkling "—so much credit for tracking down that Kirby and setting up the sting."

"Grady helped a lot, too," Molly says blushing. "With all those Internet searches. That's how we found out about Kirby's aliases."

"Yes, done on my account," Madison says dryly. "I need to change my password." She gives Grady a look and he lowers his eyes to his plate. "But for a good cause."

"The Vacuum Villain," Tanya says. "That's what I call Mr. Kirby/Bisson/Shark."

Madison's eyes widen and she shoots Tanya an appreciative glance. "That's brilliant! Why didn't you tell me that when I interviewed you? 'The Vacuum Villain'! Do you mind if I use that?"

Tanya, grinning, shakes her head. "Sure, go ahead."

Keira says, "Well, those vlogs changed our life for the better. That's for sure."

Madison's face lights up. "I'm glad. And I'm delighted by the interest in the topic. I've had more hits on those three vlogs than anything I've ever done. And I still have at least two more to do. One on the growing number of companies selling fake service dogs across the country, and another on how much real service dogs change the lives of their people for the better."

"I didn't realize that this wasn't the only case," Mrs. Franklin says. "Of fake service dogs."

"Anything good can be corrupted to make a profit," the boss pronounces, a belief he often expresses.

"But preying on people who already have problems . . ." Mrs. Franklin shakes her head. "The lowest of criminals in my book."

"Scum of the scum," Derrin says from his lawn chair off to the side, and several heads turn in surprise, then nod agreement.

Madison spoons a heap of potato salad on her plate. "Ain't it the truth! Too many people without enough training experience think they can make a fortune selling service dogs."

"And that doesn't count all the purported services dogs that are merely pets with a twenty-dollar tag bought on the Internet," Annie says. "Giving legitimate service dogs a bad name by their awful behavior in public. Are you going to do a piece on that?"

Madison gives her a wry smile. "I might, but to be honest, many of my subscribers—the ones who pay my bills—might not want to hear that side of the story. They want feel-good stories where the dogs are always heroes."

Annie sighs and shakes her head. "It's a pity," she says at last. "As a trainer, it drives me nuts to see those dogs in public."

"I think Kirby is worse," Molly says. "Charging so much for dogs who don't know how to behave at all."

More nods of agreement.

"Exactly," Madison says. "That's something my viewers can get behind."

"What about that lady at LSSC?" Keira asks, a hot dog halfway to her mouth. "Lisa Crossman. The one that stopped taking my calls and told me to quit bothering her?"

Madison gives her an appreciative look. "Makes you wonder, doesn't it? Why she would act that way. She *said* it's because she didn't have time and that the company was dealing with the issue internally. But in my investigation, I learned something interesting." A gleam comes into her eyes. "Lisa Crossman has suddenly resigned from LSSC. No one in the organization is saying why, but I've heard from one of my police sources—not your mom," she hastens to add with a glance toward Molly "—that Lisa is under investigation. Because the question we all have to ask is just how did Mr. Kirby/Bisson/Shark get the info he needed to clone the LSSC website? And the application forms?"

"They were in it together!" Molly exclaims. "Lisa and Kirby!"

Madison smiles. "Well, no one has proved it yet, but as my Daddy used to say, I think that dog will hunt."

What? Dog? Hunt? Lost me there.

"Did they know each other?" Molly asks.

Madison smiles at her. "You know what to ask. It turns out our Kirby Banes, under the name of Kerry Bisson—which might be his real name—worked briefly as a trainer at LSSC several years ago, and he and Miss Lisa were an item. But he was let go—no one is forthcoming about the reason—but one kennel cleaner I interviewed didn't think he was particularly good with the dogs."

For a moment no one speaks. Keira takes the last bite of her hot dog just as Annie says in a firm tone, "Chloe, quit begging!" With a little sigh, Chloe drops her gaze, cleans the drool from her face, and lies down.

"Since my piece ran, several people have come forward and claimed Kirby—or one his aliases—sold them untrained dogs," Madison says. "And—nothing proven yet—but it seems Kirby has had relationships with women from other kennels. Mining the source, I suspect."

Annie frowns at this. "Oh, dear. I hope this doesn't put LSSC out of business—or whatever happens to nonprofit organizations."

"Nonprofit organizations are businesses like any other, except they aren't supposed to make profits. Not that some don't do so and try to hide it." Madison sighs. "But Kirby and Lisa aside, LSSC seems legit. They have a long list of happy clients with dogs that have truly made a difference in their lives." She pauses to take a bite of potato salad and waves her fork toward Mrs. Franklin. "Delicious! I'll have to get your recipe."

"My Grandma's," Mrs. Franklin says, looking pleased.

"Anyway," Madison continues, "I'm going to profile some of those clients in my next vlog. Give LSSC some favorable publicity. Especially since they seem to be doing their best to take care of the people who got the fake dogs—" she nods at Keira "—like they did with you and your son."

More talking and more eating. I'm happy to report that Molly doesn't finish her hot dog and slips me a good-sized bite. Sadly, Chloe notices and speeds over to us, her nose practically in Molly's lap.

"Chloe, no!" Annie says firmly. With another sigh, Chloe sinks to the ground.

Kenny gets up and asks about dessert and soon the table is being cleared and pieces of cake and pie parceled out along with compliments on how good it all tastes. I wouldn't know as none of it has come my way yet, except for that bit of hot dog.

More conversation which makes dessert drag on for some time. I doze. Finally, Molly stands up, and along with several others clears the table, and at last Chloe and I get fed.

After that, my belly full from the delicious scraps Mrs. Franklin added to my kibble—and to Chloe's as well—I stretch out on the cool grass for a satisfying nap.

It is almost dark when I awake to the sound of the Franklins leaving. Somehow, Madison and Grady are already gone. Don't know how I slept through that. Keira and Jordan are heading for the gate as well, Lucy walking calmly by Jordan's side.

"Thanks for coming," Molly calls.

Keira turns and walks back to her. "Thank *you*," she says, her voice becoming husky. She steps forward and gives Molly a hug. "Thank you," she whispers again, and then abruptly turns and catches up to Jordan and Lucy.

It turns out it takes a fair amount of time to clean up after a party. Annie and Molly carry food into the kitchen while the boss collects all the trash and takes it out to the bin. He locks the gate with a new heavy-duty chain he bought right after he came back from the honeymoon. And then he goes inside, Chloe and me at his heels.

Chloe heads for my bed, but I give her a stare and she backs off and goes to her own instead. And then Moxy, evidently feeling left out, starts to yowl in the mudroom. I have to say that living with other animals has its complications.

Annie collapses on the couch, kicking her shoes off. "Well, this was a day and a half," she says.

Molly nods, dropping into the armchair beside the couch.

The boss sinks down next to Annie, draping an arm over her shoulders.

She gives him a tired smile. "But I think our first party went well. In our *own* home." She leans in to kiss him on the cheek.

The boss pulls her closer. "In our own home—if we don't count the years it'll take to pay it off."

Annie rolls her eyes. "Well, yes, that."

Molly's phone chimes. She flips it open and her face lights up. "Oh, hi, Mom," she says, hurrying through the kitchen to go outside. Normally, I'd follow, but the truth is, I'm tired from all the activity. I relax on my bed. The boss closes his eyes and somehow I do, too.

We all pop awake when Molly bustles back into the room, phone in hand. "Guess what? I know why Doodle was growling at Denzel."

"You mean other than the fact that the man's a jerk?" the boss asks, straightening up. "Although," he turns his head to give me the eye, "He still shouldn't have growled."

"Well, yeah. I just talked to Mom. She finally got the results back on the fingerprints that Tanya and I took. Guess who was in the army for a couple of years right out of high school and was fingerprinted, and whose fingerprints match the ones on the gate and the beer can?"

"Denzel?" The boss and Annie ask simultaneously.

"Yeah. He's the one who cut the chain and let Doodle out. His fingerprints were on the beer can *and* the lock."

For a moment, no one speaks.

The boss shakes his head. "I wouldn't have thought . . ."

"The only good thing is that the meat wasn't poisoned," Molly says. "Mom thinks he just wanted to lure Doodle out of the yard."

"Where he could have been hit by a car and killed," the boss says.

Seriously?

"Yeah." Molly's face clouds. "Do you think we should tell Mrs. Thomas? Mom says it's up to us whether or not we want to pursue the case."

The boss rubs his beard, not answering right away. Finally, he says, "I think Mrs. Thomas already has her share of disappointment in her son. I'm not sure we need to add to it."

Molly nods, her eyes dark. "I know. She was really sad. But what if he does it again? And we lost Doodle and Chloe?"

At the sound of her name, Chloe raises her head briefly only to lower it again and resume her nap.

Molly frowns. "Maybe instead of telling Mrs. Thomas, we should tell Denzel. If he knows *we* know, maybe he'll leave us alone. And quit bothering his mother."

Annie, sitting up now, says, "I like that."

The boss looks unsure.

"We should do it now," Molly says. "Before he thinks about trying again."

"I'm not sure I even have his number," the boss says.

"He left a card. That time he came over when Mrs. Thomas was here, remember?"

Annie says, "I think she's right—we should do it now. Although I swore I didn't want to do one more thing today."

The boss gives her a light kiss. "Okay. Don't get up." He goes into the room he calls his office and comes back holding a business card. "We'll see what Mr. Denzel Thomas has to say for himself."

He taps his phone.

"Put it on speaker," Annie says.

The grating sound becomes loud. And then, a voice says, "This is Denzel."

"Hi, Denzel." The boss's voice is friendly, but I hear the tension in it all the same. "Josh Hunter here."

"Hunter!" Denzel says. "Have you changed your mind? About the house? I could give you a great deal—"

The boss's voice turns crisp. Cold even. "I don't know if you realize we had fingerprints taken after someone cut the lock on our gate and let our dog out, but we did. And we just got the results back."

Silence.

"They match yours. Exactly. And we have a cop who is interested in pursuing the case—" he glances at Molly "—if we're willing to sign a complaint. So here's the deal we're going to give *you*. If you so much as drive by this house again, we'll sign the complaint and have you arrested. But if you leave us alone, we won't."

More silence. Finally, "What about Mama?"

"What about her?" the boss asks.

"Are you going to tell her?"

"Only if you give us—or her—any more problems about this house. So that's the deal. You stay out of our life and we'll stay out of yours. Understood?"

Silence. Then, at last, "Yeah."

"Deal?" the boss presses.

"Deal." Denzel spits out the word and then his phone goes dead.

"Well, that felt good." The boss smiles at Molly. "That was a great idea!"

"The greatest idea was taking the fingerprints in the first place," Annie says, giving Molly a thumbs up.

"True," the boss agrees. "I don't think you need to pay me back for that fingerprint kit."

Molly's face floods with color and clearly she's pleased.

Annie pushes up to her feet. "I'm going to get a shower. And go to bed early." She pads off to the bedroom, and then, clothes in hand goes into the bathroom. Pretty soon, I hear the shower start.

The boss settles on the couch, motioning for Molly to sit beside him. When she does, he puts his arm around her, pulling her close. "What did I do to deserve such a smart kid?" he asks.

Molly murmurs something, but I can't make it out.

"And not just smart, but, like Annie says, good-hearted." He releases her and twists back a little to look her in the eye. "Are you doing okay? With all these . . . changes? I know it can be hard."

Molly doesn't hesitate. "Yeah. Fine." Then, after a pause, "Well, I mean, yeah, it's been a little hard and I was worried that, I don't know, that everything would be weird. But it's not." She thinks a moment, glancing at the bathroom door. "It's nice to have Annie here. Really nice."

"Sometimes even when things are good, they can be hard," the boss suggests.

"Yeah," Molly admits. "That's what Mrs. Franklin said. Do you know what she told me? She locked herself in the bathroom and cried the day they bought their house because she was so scared. But it was one of the best things they ever did."

The boss looks surprised.

"I guess—" Molly pauses a second "—hard can be good, you know? Like dog training. Hard work sometimes but worth it."

Hey. Not sure about that! Depends on the trainer.

"And you're so much happier," Molly adds with a smile. "Less grumpy."

The boss raises his eyebrows at this, but then pulls her into another hug. "Good," he says, with relief. *"Good!"*

And then, because I feel I need to be part of this, I rush over and push my nose between them. And then Chloe sits up and barks and Moxy starts to yowl from the mudroom.

The bathroom door opens. "Is everything okay?" Annie asks, her hair dripping, and a towel wrapped around her.

"Fine!" the boss and Molly say at the same time. They look at each other and laugh.

And Molly, her eyes bright, gives Annie this really huge smile. "Everything is fine."

Authors depend upon reviews! If you enjoyed this book, please consider writing a review on your favorite retail site. It can be as short as a couple of sentences—every review helps and will be greatly appreciated!

Don't miss out! Subscribe to Susan's newsletter at *https://www.subscribepage.com/n1b5k5* for a FREE short story, advance notice for future publications and special previews available only to subscribers. Your email will never be shared and you can unsubscribe at any time.

About the Author

Susan J. Kroupa is a dog lover who adopted Shadow, the obedience-impaired labradoodle whose antics served as the inspiration for Doodle. (Read about the adventures and misadventures of raising Shadow at doodlewhacked.com.)

She is also an award-winning author whose fiction has appeared in *Realms of Fantasy*, and in a variety of professional anthologies, including *Bruce Coville's Shapeshifters*. Her nonfiction publications include features about environmental issues and Hopi Indian culture for *The Arizona Republic*, *High Country News*, and *American Forests*.

She lives in the Blue Ridge Mountains in Southwestern Virginia, where she keeps busy writing, gardening, and walking her standard poodle, Toby.

Visit her online at susankroupa.com.

Acknowledgments

First, a shout-out to all the well-trained service dogs who have enriched their humans' lives in countless ways and to the breeders, trainers, and organizations who have worked together to provide them. Your work truly makes the world a better place.

I'm grateful to Sara Frommer, Marilyn Boissonneault, and Pat Nelson for their invaluable help in proofreading the book. Thanks, too, to my ever-patient son, Joe, who helped me with both photo-editing and legal questions in this book, as he has with every book in the series.

A huge thanks to those readers and reviewers who have loved Doodle. Your comments and support have given me the heart to keep writing.

Finally, as always, thanks to Tom who makes me laugh, and makes it all worthwhile.

The Doodlebugged Mysteries

Bed-Bugged: Doodlebugged Mysteries #1

Ask Doodle why he flunked out of service-dog school and he'll tell you: smart and obedient don't always go hand in hand. Now he has a new job sniffing out bed bugs for his new boss, Josh Hunter. The best part of the job? Molly, the boss's ten-year old daughter, who slips Doodle extra treats when she's not busy snapping photos with her new camera. But Molly has secrets of her own. And when she enlists Doodle's help to solve a crime, his nose and her camera lead them straight to danger. A charming mystery for dog lovers of all ages.

Out-Sniffed: Doodlebugged Mysteries #2

Doodle's nose gets put to the test when Molly starts training him to find something very different from bed bugs to clear her best friend's brother from drug charges. But when Doodle fails to find two vials containing bed bugs during a practice for an important certification trial, the boss is furious.

It takes all of Molly's ingenuity and Doodle's keen intelligence to sniff out the real villains and set things right again.

Nominated for the Maxwell Medallion by the Dog Writers Association of America.

Dog-Nabbed: Doodlebugged Mysteries #3

A trip to the Blue Ridge Mountains quickly turns dangerous when Molly tries to help a friend and runs smack into an unscrupulous man with a big secret. And Doodle discovers that while it's no fun being lost in the woods, it can be worse to be found—by the wrong person.

Bad-Mouthed: Doodlebugged Mysteries #4

Doodle's the first to admit he doesn't get Christmas. His job is to find bed bugs for his boss's bed bug detection business and to watch over the boss's ten-year-old daughter, Molly. It is not to play a black sheep in a Christmas pageant, a lose-lose situation for sure. Not to mention that just when things start to get interesting, Doodle attracts the attention of a popular video-blogger, whose subsequent "feature" jeopardizes the boss's business.

Throw in a handful of threatening letters, a devastating fire and some lost dogs, and Molly and Doodle have their hands—well, in Doodle's case, his paws—full finding out just who's been naughty and who's been nice.

Ruff-Housed: Doodlebugged Mysteries #5

Sit. Stay. Be Polite with Strangers. What could be easier?

That's what Doodle thinks when Molly signs him up to take the Canine Good Citizen Test at the annual DogDays Fair.

But the test turns out to be no walk (or sit) in the park. Did he miss the memo about the explosions?

While Molly and her friends investigate, a dog disappears, with repercussions that threaten the bonds of an entire family.

Throw in a bullying neighbor and a chase across a squirrel-infested park near the White House, and Doodle begins to wonder if he and Molly have bitten off more than they can chew.

Winner of the 2017 Dog Writers Association of America AKC S.T.A.R. Puppy and Canine Good Citizen Award for the best writing about the AKC Canine Good Citizen Program.

Mis-Chipped: Doodlebugged Mysteries #6

One dog, two microchips, two claims . . .

When Molly and Doodle watch a good friend's dog race in flyball tournament, Doodle thinks flyball might be fun. Until the dog shows an unusual talent for the sport and someone else claims to be the dog's owner. Thrown into a world of heartless criminals and hard choices, Molly and her friend set out to find the truth. But it takes Doodle's nose, Molly's persistence, and a big dose of courage to set things right.

Ill-Served: Doodlebugged Mysteries #7

Big changes come into Molly's and Doodle's lives when the boss gets married. Doodle loves their new home, except for the annoying kitten that seems to have come with it. But then a neighbor threatens the boss, and escalating acts of vandalism make it clear that someone is trying to force them out. Worse, Molly's new friend collapses on the sidewalk after his service dog runs away. The dog is supposed to be a diabetic alert dog, but he doesn't act like any service dog Doodle has ever known. With the boss away on his honeymoon, it's up to Molly and Doodle to sniff out the truth and set things right.

Visit susankroupa.com to learn more about these and upcoming new titles.